In the sanctuary of the trees, in darkness, they touched—and a current of awareness, electric and blue-white hot, crackled between Dylan's hand and the bare flesh of Keely's shoulder . . .

"This is crazy," he muttered, awe in his voice. Then, urgently, he asked, "What's your name?"

"Keely."

"Yes." He was triumphant. "Keely is perfect. Are you pretty? I can't tell. I don't even care." He touched her face. "Oh, yes, you're beautiful."

"Your fingers lie," she whispered. "I couldn't touch beautiful with an extension ladder." Reaching up, she felt his face with both hands. "No beard. No warts."

When her fingers brushed across his lips, he moaned and dipped his head toward her. She had anticipated the kiss; she knew it was going to happen. But she didn't expect the feeling that they weren't discovering but reclaiming. There were none of the hesitant, awkward fumblings of strangers. It was instant furor, instant craving, the merging of two pairs of lips that should have been together all along. . . .

WHAT ARE *LOVESWEPT* ROMANCES?

They are stories of true romance and touching emotion. We believe those two very important ingredients are constants in our highly sensual and very believable stories in the *LOVESWEPT* line. Our goal is to give you, the reader, stories of consistently high quality that may sometimes make you laugh, sometimes make you cry, but are always fresh and creative and contain many delightful surprises within their pages.

Most romance fans read an enormous number of books. Those they truly love, they keep. Others may be traded with friends and soon forgotten. We hope that each *LOVESWEPT* romance will be a treasure—a "keeper." We will always try to publish

LOVE STORIES YOU'LL NEVER FORGET
BY AUTHORS YOU'LL ALWAYS REMEMBER

The Editors

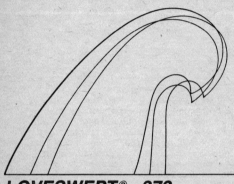

LOVESWEPT® • 372

Billie Green
Bad for Each Other

 BANTAM BOOKS
NEW YORK • TORONTO • LONDON • SYDNEY • AUCKLAND

One

So far, it was not the best day of Keely's life.

The morning had been full of trials and tribulations. A real Old Testament kind of day. For no good reason, the alarm had gone off thirty minutes late—she was positive she hadn't pushed the "Please, Please Let Me Sleep for Just Five More Minutes" button more than twice. Next, she had been able to locate only one of her favorite beige flats, which meant she had to wear the brown ones, the brown ones that pinched. Then several curls, several very conspicuous curls, had decided to go north when all the others were going south, making her look like an extra from *One Million* B.C. The next tribulation had come at the counter of a doughnut shop where Keely was manhandled by a tiny woman with pink hair and an attitude.

To top it all off, the minute after she had sat down in the cubicle she sometimes called her office, right after she had spilled coffee on her new linen skirt, her boss had been on the telephone demanding to see her immediately.

It was *not* Keely's best day.

"Inner strength, that's the ticket," she muttered as she made her way to Henry's office. It would have to be *inner* strength, because this morning the stuff on the outside wasn't going to be any help at all.

Keely had never become used to men finding her attractive. Only someone with poor vision and a good imagination would have called her pretty. Her curly hair wasn't cinnamon or copper or russet. It was just plain red. And her figure leaned more toward angular than curvy. Although she couldn't find it herself, Keely had decided there must be something in her expression, something in her easy laughter, that gave men the impression she was a little wild. Poor souls, little did they know.

"It's about time," Henry said when the door closed behind her. "Things are *happening*, Miss Durant."

Not a good sign, she thought. Henry only called her Miss Durant when his blood pressure went up.

Henry Evans, Keely's boss and the editor of *Texas Times* magazine, had hired her three years ago. Henry was a fist-pounding screamer who spent the better part of each day perfecting the art of tyranny. He saw himself as an editor of the old school, the kind who instilled slavering terror in the hearts of his employees. Henry had remarkably clear vision.

"I'm quivering with suspense," she said. "Lay it on me, *el Supremo*."

"Well, Miss Smarty Pants, while you've been fiddle-fussing around, I've been pulling off a coup. A genuine, you-bet-your-asters coup." Exhilaration radiated from his angular, normally pale face. "Regional magazines don't get chances at an interview like this . . . but *my* magazine will."

Henry was practically licking his lips. "Come on," he urged. "Guess who it is. Just take a wild guess."

There were a dozen things Keely should have been doing, dull but necessary tasks that made up 90 percent of a journalist's job. But Henry was the boss with a capital B. If he wanted to play guessing games, Keely wasn't going to argue with him.

"Couldn't you give me a hint?" she asked. "The field is rather wide." Anything that went on in the state of Texas—the good, the bad, the ridiculous—was reported in *Texas Times*. Henry's mystery interview could be with anyone. "What are we talking about?" she continued. "Politics? Religion? Business? Crime and punishment? I can't think of anyone in any of those categories who would be considered a coup."

He laughed, his gray eyes sparkling. "You forgot entertainment?"

"Patrick Swayze? Bette Midler?" she offered with a shrug. "There isn't an actor in the business who hasn't been done to death in the tabloids. Unless you've got Garbo?"

"Did I say it was an actor?" He paused, intentionally building suspense. "How does Dylan Tate grab you?"

Keely's head jerked up sharply. *Dylan Tate.* Several seconds passed before she spoke. "He's back in Dallas?" She whistled softly in awe. "Okay, I'll admit it, you've pulled off a genuine coup. That's one interview I definitely look forward to reading."

Henry studied her for a moment, then he grinned. "How about you looking forward to writing it instead?"

Keely became perfectly still. Long seconds ticked by as Henry waited for her reaction. Finally she moistened her lips and met his steady gaze. "Are you saying you want *me* to do the interview?"

"Now you're catching on."

Keely swallowed heavily. It was a good assignment. No, she amended silently, it was a great assignment. The last interview Dylan Tate had given was three years earlier, and that was a noninformative piece in *Rolling Stone.*

"Why *Texas Times*? And why me?" Keely frowned. "Are you sure you know what you're doing? I don't do music . . . or show business. I don't even know how he's classified since he made that movie. But whatever he is, he's not my thing. Why didn't you give it to Wayne? You hired him specifically to do entertainment pieces. Or am I being too logical here?"

"Anybody ever tell you you're getting too big for your britches? I didn't give it to Wayne because I don't want an entertainment piece. Besides, Wayne's biased. I think he is president of the local Dylan Tate fan club or something."

Keely chuckled. "It was a bit much when Wayne started dressing like Tate. Bless his pointed little head, he doesn't have the build for tight corduroys and turtlenecks. But that still doesn't explain why you want me to do it," she said, then a new thought occurred to her. "Did Tate ask for me? I mean, has he read my stuff and . . . and liked my style or something?"

"No, I haven't told him who's doing the interview. I don't think he really cares. The only reason he's agreed to do it is because his father was a friend of mine. We grew up together over in Fort Worth."

Henry stood up and walked around the desk, leaning his bony rump against it. "I want you to do it because of this thing you have with people. You know how to draw them out. See, I want a whole new perspective on Dylan Tate. If Wayne did the interview, we'd find out why Tate made the movie. We'd find out what it's like to be a star after years of being a virtually unknown saxophone player. We'd find out what it's like to suddenly have women hanging all over him. That's regulation stuff. Hell, we might as well interview Michael Jackson or Rod Stewart! I don't want that. I want what *you* do. I want you to dig down and find the man. This is a genuine son of Texas who made it big. I want you to get into his mind and find out what motivates him. I want his likes and dislikes, his vulnerabilities. I want his *soul*. Readers love that kind of crap." Henry's smile was a study in innocence. "You're better at it than anyone I know. You'll show us the man not as he's perceived, but as he really is. Sharp-witted or dull as dirt, sensitive or brutal. You'll find out if he couldn't stand his mamma. If he had the hots for his third-grade teacher." He waved a hand vigorously. "Whatever's there, you'll find it. You'll have him spilling his guts. And you'll make sure he loves every minute of it."

She grimaced. "You're just oozing with the milk of human kindness, aren't you? And you say his father was a friend of yours?"

"What does that have to do with anything?" Henry looked genuinely bewildered. "Are you gonna take this job or not?" He straightened in exasperation. "I can't make you out. Any other writer on staff—hell, any writer in the business—would be on his knees kissing my feet for a chance at this assignment."

She glanced down at Henry's feet. The original shape and color of his track shoes had been lost somewhere in the dim mists of time. "Can't I just say thank you very much?"

Henry smiled in satisfaction. "That's more like it." He pushed away from the desk and returned to his chair. "Now get out of here. I'll let you know when I have everything set up."

As Keely walked away from Henry's office, she

paid no attention to where she was going, and she didn't consciously take in the people, her co-workers, who stared at her when she failed to acknowledge them.

She didn't want Henry's assignment. She wanted someone else to pull off his coup. It wasn't her kind of thing at all. Only two days before, Keely had finished an interview with two elderly women who had been thrown in jail for contempt of court because they had wanted to protect a friend. They were confused and scared, but they were also stubborn and loyal. Good people. The type Keely enjoyed writing about.

If there was a Keely Durant trademark, it was her focus on real people, the kind who represented 90 percent of the population of the world; people who did their best to survive in a world over which they had no control. She wrote about the tragedies and triumphs of the average Texan. She sought out ordinary folks who sometimes managed to overcome extraordinary odds.

Dylan Tate didn't fit into that category. The man could have been in the pilot program for *Lifestyles of the Rich and Famous*. He was the last person Keely would have chosen to interview, but the choice hadn't been hers to make. Henry had given her the assignment because he believed in her ability. He thought she would do a better job than anyone else on staff. Keely couldn't let him down. She would grit her teeth and do it. She would do it for Henry.

Oh, please, she thought, swallowing a semihysterical giggle. *Now I'm thinking in dialogue from a bad forties movie. "Go out and do it for the chief."*

In truth, Henry's faith in her was only one of the reasons Keely had accepted the assignment. Among other things, she had accepted it because it was her job. A story was a story was a story.

When she reached the library, a large room on the floor below her office-slash-cubicle, Keely pulled a thick folder from a metal cabinet and carried it to a Formica-topped table. For a long time she sat staring at the closed file. Finally she took a deep breath and opened it. The folder was crammed full of newspaper and magazine clippings. And pictures. There were dozens of photographs taken from various magazines and newspapers.

She picked up a picture that lay on top of the pile. It was small and was attached to an even smaller article dated fifteen years earlier. Dylan Tate would have been twenty-two. Although the celebrity-watching public had yet to discover him, according to the article, Dylan Tate already had a growing audience of hard-core blues aficionados.

Keely brought the fuzzy picture closer to her face. Was it her imagination, or could she actually see the beginning of cynicism in his dark eyes? Laying the photograph aside, she continued to sort through the pile. There were a few reviews in which some obscure critic would throw around words like "genius" or "new king of the blues." At a time when most of the American public had never heard of Dylan Tate, his concerts and club engagements were always well reviewed. He had been quietly making a name for himself in the world of music.

Then came the movie *Sligh,* and suddenly Tate was no longer an obscure musical genius. He was a superstar.

The movie had been the sleeper hit of the summer. It told the story of Ralph Sligh, a saxophone player working in a run-down club in West Texas. The camera had followed Sligh's life, documenting his decline as he was devastated first by the philandering of his wife, then by the death of his young son. In graphic detail, the film showed how Sligh's music had pulled him back from the brink of insanity.

Sligh had received critical and popular acclaim. The experts agreed that the acting, directing, and cinematography were uniformly superb. But it wasn't the artistic excellence that had made the movie a hit with the general public. One scene had done that.

Keely remembered every detail. Vividly. She had been affected by it as much as every other woman in the country. The scene opened with a view of the vast West Texas night sky, then closed in on a lone figure in the bed of an ancient pickup. Sligh sat with his back against the cab. His chest and feet were bare, and his tight corduroy jeans had been left undone at the waist. One knee was raised to support the saxophone he held with both hands. His dark brown hair was long and unkempt, his face ravaged by recent experiences.

For a moment he sat listening to the howl of a lone dog, then he let his saxophone react to the sound. After a short while, he stopped. Seconds later the distant wail of a police siren reached him, and the saxophone echoed the lonely, anxious sound. Soon scenes from his life began to play through his mind, and he reacted to each memory with music. Finally he heard, from the distance of the past, a child laughing, calling to him. He played feverishly, hellish notes that seemed to have no end. Perspiration covered his chest and face as he played and played. There was guilt and anger and loss in the music. There was immeasurable agony in his face. The scene became a wall of solid pain that no one in the audience could withstand. Viewers cried for him and with him.

For months the movie was on everyone's lips. The movie and Dylan Tate. Thousands of women— even women who in the past had dismissed the blues as that music played in New Orleans—became instant fans of the art. They chose Dylan Tate as their hero, the man to star in their fantasies. Each and every one came away from the movie wanting to hold him and comfort him until he was well enough to think of other, more physical things. In a few short minutes, Dylan Tate had become the inspiration of a million hot dreams. Even though he had portrayed a disturbed, injured man, there had been a look of untamed sexuality about him. Women burned to know if he was as good as their fantasies.

Overnight Dylan Tate was the most talked-about man in the country. The movie led to his first LP, *Blues Spoken Here*, which went platinum within two weeks. The publicity was massive. Keely thumbed through picture after picture—Tate with movie stars and politicians; with millionaires and sports figures. And with women. Lots of women, and rarely the same woman twice. There were blondes, brunettes, and redheads. Sleekly sophisticated women and outrageously sexy women. He seemed to have no preference in nationality or occupation or level of intelligence. Beauty seemed the only thing the women had in common.

Then, little more than a year after *Sligh* was released, Tate abruptly stopped dating and, at the same time, stopped giving interviews. Of course, that hadn't stopped the publicity. Every move he made was watched and reported. There were pictures of him caught off guard outside clubs and restaurants. There were bird's-eye shots of him climbing out of the pool at his California home. Only now, after three years, had the publicity begun to taper off.

Maybe that's why he granted the interview, she thought with a wry laugh. Maybe he missed all the attention.

"Why are you drooling over pictures of Mr. Oh-my-God-he's-sexy Tate? Just turn around, and you can drool over a real-life love god."

Keely swung around to find a chubby blond man standing behind her, reading over her shoulder. Love god wasn't too far off, she decided. Wayne Roberts looked like an overdressed Cupid.

When Keely first came to work for *Texas Times*, Wayne along with several other men on staff, had pursued her. She had given the others a cold shoulder, but Wayne was different. He was vulnerable. It had taken some high-quality maneuvering on her part to convince him that she needed a friend, not a lover.

"When did you become starstruck?" Wayne asked, then his eyes narrowed. "What are you doing with the Tate file? Violet said you were in with Henry this morning. Now here you are, going through . . . He's given you Tate, hasn't he? If Henry wants a feature story about Tate's return to Dallas, I can do it with one hand tied behind my back. I have sources. I can talk to people who know him. Why did he give it to you?"

"Wayne, you're whining." She stood up and patted his plump shoulder. "I didn't want this assignment, but Henry didn't give me a choice. He just dumped it on me."

"You don't do entertainment. That's what they hired me for."

"That's exactly what I said." She shrugged. "If it had been an entertainment piece, Henry would have given it to you. There's no one better qualified. But he wants to focus on the personal angle."

"You mean he wants fluff? Human-interest garbage that keeps the housewives satisfied?" When Keely raised one arched brow, he blushed. "I don't mean your stuff. You do in-depth character studies."

"So diplomatic." She laughed. "That's what Henry wants, an in-depth character study. No show business. No music background."

"Oh." Wayne rubbed his chin. "I was going to catch Tate's meeting with the mayor this afternoon, but now I guess—"

"I didn't hear about that." Her brow creased with thought. "Listen, there's no reason you can't still cover it. You can add it to your personal file or use it in your 'What's Happening in Entertainment' column."

"I was just about to say that myself."

"Sure you were. Why don't I go along with you? Just as an observer," she added quickly. "I can get a look at Tate . . . and I can watch you work. I've always wanted to do that."

Wayne's chest swelled, and he suddenly looked taller. He really was a sweetheart, she thought as she followed him out of the library.

As soon as they arrived at city hall, Wayne forgot all about Keely and the article she was working on. He and the other reporters gathered on the steps of city hall speculated about Tate's decision to move back to Dallas. No one had ever unraveled his mind's workings. They only knew what he allowed them to see. It was the private man Henry wanted Keely to uncover. Henry wanted to disassemble Dylan Tate and expose all the fragile gears and sprockets.

A story is a story is a story.

They had been in front of city hall for half an hour when the crowd around Keely began to surge forward. She withstood the movement and pulled back into the shadows. Today she only wanted a distant look at Dylan Tate. She wasn't interested in throwing questions at the public man.

Flashbulbs popped all around her, and television cameras rolled. Tate accepted the key to the city and moved forward to speak into the microphone. Watching, Keely wiped sweaty palms on her skirt and moistened suddenly dry lips. His dark brown hair was still long. It wasn't slovenly or unkempt; it was just long enough to add a touch of wildness to his looks. Today there were no tight jeans. He wore pleated brown slacks and an oversized shirt the color of ripe wheat that was tucked in loosely. The shirt was only half-buttoned, and the sleeves were rolled up, exposing his forearms.

The clothes were as sexual as the ones he had worn in *Sligh,* but Keely knew he could have been wearing astronaut gear, and it would have made no difference. The way he moved, the way he held himself, made even the strongest woman catch her breath.

But sensuality wasn't all there was to Dylan Tate. Some men carried with them an aura, a certain electrifying charisma, that dimmed the personalities of everyone around them. A few politicians had it. Some evangelists and actors had it. Dylan Tate had it. In abundance.

As she stood watching, Keely wondered what all these clamoring people would think if she told them their superstar had once been involved with a small-potatoes journalist. What would they think if she told them their idol, the man who had had affairs with some of the most glamorous women in the world, used to be in the habit of leaving teeth marks on the inside of that same journalist's thigh?

Two

Keely sat at the table in the small kitchen of her apartment. With her chin resting on one hand, she stared with fierce concentration into a glass of pink lemonade. Periodically she thumped the side of the glass in an effort to sink an ice cube that had become lodged on top of two others. Her irritation grew as the lump of ice refused to budge, so she thumped harder, sending the glass skidding across the table.

When the doorbell rang, she didn't look away from the now-distant glass of lemonade. "It's not locked!" she yelled, then muttered to herself, "Cool move, mush-for-brains. It could be a door-to-door salesman." She grabbed the glass and poked viciously at the intractable ice cube. "It could be a door-to-door mass murderer."

Seconds later a tall, strongly built brunette appeared in the doorway leading from the living room. "What do you mean, 'It's not locked'? What if it had been a sex-starved psychopath?"

Keely returned her gaze to the lemonade. "Mrs. Browning across the hall sees every person who comes in or out of this apartment, day or night, rain or shine. And she can spot incipient sex from a hundred yards off. Why do you think I don't have affairs?"

Celeste Childs sat down opposite Keely. "You don't have affairs because you're Pearl Pureheart. You're an anachronism who should have lived back in the fifties, before virtue became synonymous with sexual dysfunction."

Keely raised her head and stared at her friend. "Why are you here?"

"It's Tuesday."

Keely frowned and glanced at her watch. "Is it?"

"Keely, that isn't a calendar watch. There's nothing on it but two hands and a lot of dots. You're losing it, pal." Celeste rose to her feet. "My car or yours?"

"Yours. On my way home from work I kept having to fight an urge to run down pedestrians."

"That sounds like my line. What happened to Miss Sunshine? Are we a little testy?" Celeste said as they left Keely's apartment.

"No, we're downright manic, so don't push it."

"Bad day?"

"You could say that." Keely's lips twitched in a wry smile. "You could even say cataclysmic."

Although Celeste drove all the way to the restaurant without asking a single question, Keely knew her friend wasn't through with her. The questions would come later.

Keely was prepared for that. Although it was warped, although it bordered on the masochistic, Keely found herself looking forward to Celeste's interrogation with the same wincing anticipation that accompanied the removal of a hangnail—you know it's going to hurt like hell, but a peculiar satisfaction is gained in ripping it off anyway.

A cloud of noisy good cheer absorbed the two women as soon as they walked through the door of their usual Tuesday night restaurant. They followed the hostess past a table where a group of employees had gathered around a table to sing "Happy Birthday" to a young, attractive man.

Celeste glared at the people at the birthday table. Celeste always glared. She was a world-class glarer. When they were seated, their orders taken, and their drinks served, the brunette began her tirade. Tirading was another thing Celeste was good at.

"I *hate* cute people." Celeste made no attempt to modulate her deep voice. "I look at them and I want to squash them under my size nines. I want to make them dress in discount-store clothes and get bad haircuts. I want to grab them by their crisp little collars and say, 'For heaven's sake, this is life! This counts! Precious is not a worthwhile goal.' "

Celeste's green eyes burned with a zealot's fire. "Our generation is really scary, Keely. The earth isn't going to be inherited by the meek; it's going to be inherited by hordes of bubbling, chirping cheerleaders."

Keely picked up a glass the size of a soup bowl and took a sip of her margarita. "Why do we always come here?" she asked, undisturbed by her friend's passionate harangue. "You say the same thing every Tuesday. This place hasn't changed. It always looks like an explosion in an adorable factory, and it always will. So why don't we go somewhere else?"

"We come here because I like to gripe and—"

Celeste broke off when an enormous plate of nachos was delivered by a cute young man wearing tight shorts. When he finished bubbling and chirping, Celeste studied the effect of his retreating buttocks, then continued.

"And because I like the food. And because I still don't have a date for Saturday. The only antidote for a dateless weekend is a monumental intake of calories." Celeste paused with a nacho halfway to her mouth. "When are you going to tell me about your day? Did Henry trash your story?"

"No, he liked it . . . at least, he said it was competent journalism. That's as good as it's going to get with Henry."

"Then what gives? It's got to be something pretty gruesome, or you wouldn't have ridden, of your own free will, in the Beetle from Hell." When Keely didn't answer, Celeste dropped her nacho and leaned forward. "Okay, what is it, Keely? I definitely don't like the way you look."

"Don't tell me I'm getting cute."

"Come on, cut the bull. What happened? You had this same . . . this same *desperate weirdness* about you when we first met. You looked haunted. Or hunted. You were fighting something. Like every breath you took was a punch thrown at an invisible opponent."

Keely smiled. That was exactly how it had felt, a constant fight to get through the day-to-day job of existing.

"When I first met you," Keely said quietly, "a two-year relationship had just been . . . extinguished. I felt— Oh, I don't know how to explain it. I felt cast adrift. If that sounds melodramatic, it's because it *felt* melodramatic. It was as though I'd been thrown into an unfamiliar world, a world I wasn't sure I wanted to be in."

"Relationship?" Celeste pounced on the word. "As in emotional? As in sexual? You've been holding out on me. All this time I've thought of you as a virgin with a capital V." Celeste raised one thick eyebrow. "He must have been something to get you to drop your . . . um, guard."

Keely inhaled slowly. "He was something, all right."

"Five years ago," Celeste said. "You must have still been in college."

"My second year." She smiled. "I loved college.

Not just expanding my thoughts and goals, but the people I met. People from all over the world. You don't meet many new people in Tomball."

Celeste gave a loud snort of laughter. "I'm sorry. I can't help it. Every time you say that, it just hits me the wrong way. Nobody comes from Tomball, Texas."

"I do," she said, her voice stubbornly loyal. "And it's a wonderful place. I loved growing up there. But it's like all small towns, a little insulated, a little smug. When you're young, you think the whole world is exactly like the people in your neighborhood."

"Talk about culture shock. Dallas must have been a surprise."

"I told you. I loved it. There was so much—"

"Hold on. You're getting offtrack. You're supposed to be telling me about this hot affair you had."

Hot affair? Yes, Keely decided, that was probably as good a description as any. "I'm getting there. One of the friends I made in college was Sandra Ellis. Remember, I introduced you to her a couple of years ago?"

Celeste wrinkled her nose and squinted her eyes as though she were squeezing the memory from her brain. "In Neiman-Marcus? We were tourists, she was obviously a resident. She had platinum hair, shiny enough to blind you, and spent a lot of time moaning because her size-four designer jeans were getting too tight. And she was cute," Celeste finished in disgust.

Keely laughed. "Your memory is too good. Anyway, during my second year at college Sandra invited me to spend spring break with her family. They have a place on Lake Ray Hubbard." She sighed. "I loved it. Every day was full of swimming, sailing, shopping, or just lying around doing nothing. Then Sandra's parents decided to throw a party."

Although Sandra had wanted to duck out on the party, Keely had looked forward to it. She enjoyed watching people, and she seldom had the chance to watch the glamorous types who lived in Sandra's world. Nothing Keely owned would have been right for the social set on Lake Ray Hubbard, so she bought a new dress especially for the party. It was a simple design, almost a backless slip, but it was lavender, which made her skin look translucent, and it was silk, which made her feel sensuous and beautiful . . . as long as she stayed away from mirrors.

For most of the night Keely walked around, pretending to mingle so the Ellises wouldn't worry about her. Then, without warning, the night, the party, and her life changed.

Like the other guests, Keely had been politely nibbling at the catered food. But she loved food. She adored food. And nibbling didn't do justice to the wondrous display. Seafood in exotic sauces, vegetables dressed up in party clothes. And the desserts! Her stomach whimpered in self-pity every time she glanced at the table.

It was a genuine dilemma. She couldn't embarrass Sandra and her parents by hovering over the table, but ignoring the food would be criminal neglect. She decided she would have to hide. She would fill a plate—if anyone looked at her funny, she would say it was for her boyfriend, since men were allowed to make pigs of themselves—then she would go somewhere private and eat until she could eat no more.

It didn't take long for her to discover that on this evening "somewhere private" didn't exist in the Ellis house. The place was overflowing with people. Guests wandered in and out of every room. Even the bedrooms upstairs weren't free of traffic.

That was when Keely had a flash of brilliance. Go to the wilds, she told herself. She would grab a flashlight and head for the frontier. Past the terrace and the pool. Past the tennis court. Getting back to nature was an idea whose time had come.

Therefore, half an hour later Keely sat in the midst of nature. Actually she sat on a marble bench under a carefully pruned cottonwood, but it was as close to natural as she was going to get on the Ellises' grounds. She leaned back against the smooth trunk and made muffled noises of pleasure as she ate.

"Oh, good, you brought a flashlight."

Startled, she swung the beam of light in the direction of the voice. Whoever he was, he was tall. The light caught his chest and the filled plate in his hands.

"I saw you leaving with the booty and decided

you had the right idea. I need food, but it's a little tough trying to eat with your hostess and a half-dozen of her friends breathing down your neck, isn't it?"

"I don't think anyone was clamoring to get near me," she said doubtfully. "Unless they were clamoring very quietly. I came out here because I was tired of taking polite little samples."

He laughed. "I love women who are enthusiastic eaters." He paused. "Actually I love women period, but there's something profoundly sensual about a woman who enjoys food."

"Think so?" Keely said through a mouthful of shrimp. "In that case, it's a good thing it's dark. The sauce running down my chin would probably make you my slave for life."

He laughed. He had a nice laugh. And a nice voice. It was slightly primitive, a rough edge on his personality that hadn't been smoothed away by civilized society.

"Were we introduced?" he asked as he sat down beside her. "I think I would remember your voice, but there were so many people."

"I don't know." She paused. "You're not the man who exports defective tennis shoes to Third World nations, are you?"

"No. Does that count against me?"

"Only if I were into ruthless businessmen, which I'm not."

"That's—" He broke off. "What *is* this? Shine the light over here for a second."

She turned the flashlight toward his plate and

leaned closer to see what was on his fork. "It's either calamari," she said, "or very old pasta."

"You're right. It's calamari . . . in an interesting sauce."

"I'll take it," she said, reaching out to pluck the squid from his fork. "I *am* into interesting things."

"Then you came to the wrong party."

"What's wrong with the party?"

"You've got to be kidding. Have you listened to any of those people? It doesn't matter if they're talking about world events, politics, religion, or the newest diet fad, every word they say has only one purpose behind it: to show how much money they have. To demonstrate that their possessions are better than the possessions of the person they're talking to."

She was silent for a moment. "That sounds a little smug. I take it you don't have a lot of possessions."

"Sure I have, but I don't go round telling people about them. I acquire things because they please me, not to one-up anybody. And if I sounded smug, it's because I am. I'm tickled to death that I'm not a jerk."

She heard the amusement in his voice and knew he wasn't taking the conversation seriously. It didn't matter. A debate, even a mock-debate, always stirred her blood.

"You can't lump them all together like that," she objected. "The thing to remember is, you have to leave your gavel at home. This is America. People have the inalienable right to be as nice or as nasty as they want."

"Or as superficial?"

"That too, but I still think you're judging too soon. They may seem superficial, but their emotions are real enough."

He gave a short bark of laughter. "You can't tell me that woman with the carefully streaked blond hair has ever had a real emotion in her life."

"Streaked blond hair? Oh, you mean the one wearing a green, floaty dress and big tinted glasses? I met her." Keely turned toward him in her enthusiasm. "Now I've got you. She's a perfect example of what I'm talking about. When she was explaining how a woman she detested had copied the decor of her beach house, there was genuine anguish in her face. Anguish is anguish. She felt despair just as deeply, just as keenly, as a woman trying to raise three kids on her own who suddenly loses her job."

"That's asinine."

"Maybe, but it's also human."

He chuckled. "You haven't really proven anything except that you're nicer than I am."

She shook her head. "Un-uh. Not nicer, more objective. I'm a writer . . . at least, I will be . . . A journalist has to be objective or she can't get the truth to the people."

"But a journalist has the opportunity to influence thousands of people. Shouldn't she take the opportunity to sway public opinion and right some wrongs?"

"Wrong in whose opinion? The journalist's?"

"Why not?"

"You're making a lot of assumptions. That the journalist is an okay person morally. That she is intelligent. That she has no axes to grind. What you're talking about is done all the time, but it shouldn't happen. People should be given the facts, then be allowed to make up their own minds." She paused. "You have to remember, I'm speaking from a distance. When I'm actually there and I'm dealing with a subject I care about, I don't know how I'll feel."

"You're not only idealistic, you're honest."

"Is that another way of saying I'm naive and a little backward?"

He laughed. "No, it's another way of saying you're refreshing. And even if I shouldn't make the judgment, classier than anyone back there on the terrace."

"If you don't like the people here, why did you come?"

"I'm not as idealistic as you. Or as honest. I came here to brownnose some influential people. 'Patrons of the Arts'—in caps and quotes."

Her interest, already piqued, quickened. "You're an artist?"

"I'm a saxophone player. Our hosts and several of the guests are putting together a music exposition at the museum. They're going to educate the public and let them 'experience' different forms of music. I'm in charge of the blues presentation."

"Blues? As in a harmonica, a guitar, and a fat man who whines?"

"Philistine." There was more amusement than annoyance in his rough voice. "Come to the exposition and get yourself educated."

"I might do that," she murmured as she took a forkful of something that tasted vaguely of chocolate. "I might just do that."

They sat on the marble bench a foot away from each other and talked about his chosen profession, and hers. They talked about his tastes in books and philosophy and food, and hers. His voice came to her through the warm night and held her fast with its husky power. It was a dark brown voice. A voice to savor, to roll around in the mind before allowing it to be absorbed. And as they talked, Keely forgot about the party. She even forgot about the food. Although he was cynical, he was also intelligent and grudgingly fair. He teased her a little about her ideals, but he never made them seem adolescent.

It seemed strange to reveal so many intimate thoughts and yet not be able to see him, and she was dying of curiosity but couldn't help thinking it would be rude, an invasion of his privacy, to shine the flashlight directly in his face. Keely couldn't judge his age. There was maturity in his voice, but that told her nothing. Maturity happened in the late twenties and lasted until death. He could have been twenty-six or sixty.

Finally she decided she didn't need to know how old he was or what he looked like. He made her laugh, and she felt comfortable with him. That was all she needed to know.

"I guess I should get back," he said after a while. "I don't want to. This is a much better party, but I don't think I could explain that to my hostess. Will you come back and dance with me?"

"You just want to use me to keep the talkers off you."

He laughed. "Among other things."

They moved together through the shadows of the cultivated jungle, as comfortable with silence as they had been with words. Just before they left the sanctuary of the trees, he put his hand on her shoulder and turned her toward him. "You want to hear something really—"

He broke off abruptly as a current of awareness, electric and blue-white hot, crackled between his hand and the bare flesh of her shoulder.

"Son of a bitch," he whispered, not hiding the awe in his voice.

Keely caught her breath. She had never felt anything like it. It blew her away. It weakened and strengthened at the same time.

She almost laughed aloud at the irony of it. She was finally physically attracted to a man, and she didn't even know what he looked like. What if he had an Abe Lincoln beard? What if he had an Abe Lincoln wart? It would be just like life to play a trick like that on her.

"It's the craziest thing," he murmured, then his voice grew urgent. "What's your name?"

"Keely."

"Yes." The word was triumphant. "Keely is good. Keely is perfect. Are you pretty? I can't tell. I don't even care." He touched her face. "Oh, yes, you're beautiful."

"Your fingers lie," she whispered, a hoarse laugh catching in her throat. "I couldn't touch beautiful with an extension ladder." Reaching up, she felt his face with both hands. His flesh was firm, unlined. "No beard. No warts."

When her fingers brushed across his lips, he moaned and dipped his head toward her. She had anticipated the kiss; she knew it was going to happen, and she expected it to be a superior kind of kiss. What she didn't expect was the feeling that they weren't discovering, they were reclaiming. There were none of the hesitant, awkward fumblings of two strangers trying to learn each other's preferences. It was instant furor, instant craving, the merging of two pairs of lips that should have been together all along.

When he moved his mouth to her neck, then her shoulders, she shoved her arms beneath his jacket, straining to get closer. "What's your name?" she asked, hearing the same urgency in her voice that had been in his.

"Dylan."

"Dylan," she repeated, finding deep pleasure in the name. "It sounds like you feel. Like you taste.

I'm glad you're not old enough to be my grandfather . . . but it wouldn't matter, would it?"

"No, it wouldn't matter a bit," he whispered hoarsely, and grasped her face to bring her lips back to his.

Long, sweet minutes later, when they finally reached the terrace, the light and the noise seemed harsh and intrusive. The party and the people didn't belong in the new world Keely had discovered.

She stood two feet away from him, finally able to see what before she had only felt. She stared up at him, ignoring the other guests who flowed anonymously around them.

He was different. Different from any man she had ever seen. At first she thought he was spectacularly handsome, then she realized he wasn't at all. He had irregular features, and there was an awkwardness about the way they were arranged. But some inner force, a force of incredible strength, made any ordinary measure of male beauty invalid.

The way he stood, the hard strength in his face, the knowledge in his gray eyes, matched what she had heard in his voice. "You've done more living than I have," she murmured, still gazing up at him. " You've seen things that I haven't seen and felt things that I haven't felt, will probably never see or feel."

He didn't respond. He simply stared with intense concentration at her face. "You were right. You're not beautiful. You make beautiful seem common. Blue eyes were never this blue. You're dazzling . . . and sexy as hell. But you're too young. Too bright-and-shiny new." There was no disappointment in his voice. He was simply stating a fact. "We're wrong for each other," he said. "Totally wrong, and sweet heaven, I wish we were back in the trees."

"Yes." Her voice was breathless. "Yes, so do I."

They danced. Then they danced again. And again. She didn't want to leave him. She didn't ever want to be out of his arms. The world had changed. It was made different by his presence. It had become sweeter, more poignantly alive, simply because he existed.

Before they left each other, they arranged to meet the next day, and that night, as she lay awake in the Ellises' guest room, Keely knew without a doubt that something important had happened between them. And because she had never experienced anything like it, she hadn't given a thought to resisting. . . .

"I should have remembered Newton and his apple tree," she said now, smiling grimly at Celeste. "What goes up, sooner or later, has to hit the ground again."

Remembering his kiss, the way she had felt in his arms, she shook her head. "But even if I had thought of Newton, it wouldn't have mattered. I would have gone with him that first night, even before I knew his name."

Celeste fanned her flushed face with a cocktail napkin. "I can't believe you kept all this a secret. The man sounds absolutely gorgeous."

"That's a good word. He was that and a whole lot more."

"Do you ever see him? Have I met him? What did you say his name was?"

"No, I don't see him, and I'm sure you haven't met him." She paused. "His name is Dylan . . . Dylan Tate."

Celeste laughed. "You're kidding. A saxophone player named Dylan Tate? That's freaky." She frowned. "Wait a minute. That's too freaky. There couldn't be two—" Celeste stopped talking abruptly. She gasped, choked, grabbed her water, then choked again. "Dylan . . . *Dylan Tate.* That's what you said, wasn't it? You can't mean *the* Dylan Tate?"

"The one and only."

Celeste leaned back in her chair and stared at Keely as though she had never seen her before. As though, in minutes, she had become a different person.

"Stop looking at me like that," Keely said in irritation. "You act like I've grown horns or something. Like I must have hidden depth if Dylan Tate once wanted me."

"No . . . no," her friend denied. "I've always known you were deep. . . . it's just that— It would probably be unforgivably crude if I asked, you know, what he was like in— No, forget I said that. That's really disgusting. I can't believe I was actually going to ask."

If it hadn't meant so much, Keely would have told Celeste what she was dying to know. She would have told her that in bed Dylan Tate was what every woman dreamed of. He was more than mere imagination could conjure. In bed.

"You don't have to say anything," Celeste said. "Just looking at your expression leaves me short of breath." She paused. "Why haven't you told me before? And why are you telling me now?"

"I didn't tell you because I didn't want to talk about it . . . then. It was over. I didn't want the memories out in the open. I was trying to forget and get on with my life."

"So why are you telling me now?" Celeste repeated.

Keely glanced away, staring into the distance, then she pulled her gaze reluctantly back to Celeste's. "Henry gave me a new assignment today. An interview."

The color drained from Celeste's face before coming back in a rush. "With . . . with *him*?"

Keely nodded, then swallowed the rest of her drink.

"Oh my gosh...oh my gosh." Celeste breathed in awe. "How old am I? Why do I feel like a thirteen-year-old who's just caught a glimpse of Michael Jackson? Like any minute I'm going to start screaming and crying. Oh my gosh, you're actually going to interview—" She broke off. Her face changed as knowledge dawned. "Oh. My. Gosh. What are you going to do? Have you seen him since you broke up?"

Keely shook her head. "He moved to New York. Then, after *Sligh*, he stayed in California."

"Shouldn't you tell your boss? Somehow it seems like pertinent information. Was the breakup friendly or hostile?"

Keely raised one brow. "Ever see *Apocalypse Now*?"

"That bad, huh?" She grimaced. "Do you think he'll get nasty and refuse to let you do the interview?"

"No," Keely said without hesitation, "he's not like that. It will be uncomfortable. It will be—" She broke off and shook her head. "I don't know why I didn't tell Henry. I guess I should have."

"Maybe you want to see *him* again. Yumpin' Yiminy, who wouldn't? Maybe you wanted to see if the bells will still ring and the rockets explode."

Keely laughed. "That won't happen. It's all over. Five years over."

"Maybe the love is over," Celeste said, "but don't forget about that old devil sex."

Keely shook her head. "All gone."

"What if you're wrong? What if you see him and it's all still there?"

"I'm not wrong."

"But if you are?"

"It would make no difference," she said slowly. "I wouldn't go back. He made me crazy. I made him crazy. We were totally wrong for each other. No, not just wrong. Bad. We were bad for each other. We became people we didn't like when we were together. It was like in chemistry class. You take two perfectly harmless ingredients, combine them, and you get something destructive. That's how it was with us. Individually we're nice people, but put us together and you get an explosion every time."

Keely sat up straighter, shaking loose from the mood that had fallen on her. "At least, that's the way it used to be. It's all gone now. I looked at him today, and I saw Dylan Tate, superstar. I couldn't find my Dylan, the man I . . . the man I was so attracted to. There was no feeling left in me for this new Dylan. I wasn't even mad at him anymore. All the emotion—the love, the desire, even the anger—all that was burned out of both of us a long time ago. It is absolutely, positively gone."

Three

There is no feeling left in me for this new Dylan.
It is absolutely, positively gone.

As she drove, Keely repeated the words over and over in her head. The words were a tautological litany, a fervent whisper in the ears of the gods.

It was seven-thirty in the morning, and her destination was a small café in north Dallas. Two men waited for her there. Henry and Dylan. As of the evening before, Henry had not seen fit to tell Dylan who his interviewer would be. As of the present moment, Keely had not seen fit, due to a serious deficiency in pluck, to tell Henry that she knew Dylan Tate.

Had it been wishful thinking when she told Celeste that Dylan wouldn't get nasty? There had been more than anger the last time they saw each other. He could get nasty as hell this time. If he was into grudges. If he was not quite as adult as Keely was.

Adult? she thought wryly. What kind of adult spends four hours trying to decide what to wear? What kind of adult throws her brush out the window because her hair doesn't look like Candice Bergen's? So maybe she wasn't as adult as she had hoped, she conceded silently. And if she wasn't, there was no guarantee Dylan would be.

She should have told Henry. It would have been tough, but she could have found a way. Keely dealt with words every day. She could have pulled up a few and phrased the truth in a way that wouldn't have embarrassed her.

Henry, there's one small detail I forgot to mention. The fact is, Dylan Tate and I used to . . . uh . . . know each other.

Too biblical?

Henry, because of a past association, there is a possibility some slight tension might exist between me and our subject.

Too ambiguous?

Henry, Dylan Tate and I once had a flaming affair and now he hates my guts and this meeting could have unanticipated results, including but not limited to Dylan screaming at me, punching you out, and suing the magazine.

She giggled. The thought of Henry ducking Dylan's punches made her feel better. It would almost be worth all the worry. Almost.

For once traffic on Central ran smoothly, and

minutes later Keely parked behind the café and stepped out of her red Toyota. She stood for a moment, smoothing the skirt of her blue sundress. Then her hands went to her hair to perform the same operation. It was purely a nervous gesture, because her shoulder-length red curls would not be smoothed.

After she had thrown her brush out the window, Keely had given up on her hair and had used two gold clips to pull it high on each side of her head. She had told herself that this was the best she was going to look, and the thought had made her angry. Angrier. Only the fact that the mirror was too big to throw out the window had saved it from following the brush.

It shouldn't have mattered. She was going to an interview, not an audition. The problem was, Keely wasn't used to running into her old lovers. Put all her old lovers together and they didn't exactly make a crowd. Put her all her old lovers together and they didn't exactly make two. There had only ever been Dylan. He was the only man she had let get close to her. And considering the gruesome results, she hadn't been overly anxious to try again with another man. One Armageddon per lifetime was all the heart could stand.

Inside the café she stood for a moment, her heart racing, her nerves taut, as she scanned the tables for the two men. She finally located them at a corner table. Henry sat facing the door, his thin arms on the table. Beside him, Dylan leaned forward in conversation, only visible in profile. He was dressed casually: dark sunglasses, lightweight jacket, a pale green shirt with several buttons left undone.

Keely's pulse slowly returned to normal as relief spread through her. It was Dylan Tate, the superstar. She didn't know this Dylan, and a stranger couldn't affect her one way or the other.

She walked toward the table, forcing confidence and purpose into her steps. Henry saw her first and reluctantly rose to his feet, reluctantly because Henry seldom remembered she was a woman. When she drew nearer, she glanced at Dylan, who had also stood up. She saw no reaction on the superstar's face, but that didn't mean anything. Even the Dylan she remembered had never given anything away in his expression.

"It's about time, Durant," Henry said as she reached them. "I thought I said eight sharp."

Keely didn't glance at her watch. She knew it couldn't have been more than two minutes after eight. "Heavy traffic," she lied with a shrug.

Henry glanced at Dylan. "Dylan, Keely . . . Keely, Dylan. Now everybody sit down and let's get this thing moving."

No one would ever accuse Henry of making idle chatter. Or of possessing social graces. Keely glanced at Henry, then at Dylan. Two things were immediately apparent. Henry had told Dylan that Keely was doing the interview. And Dylan hadn't told Henry a thing. If he had, Henry would have chewed her up and spit her out the second she had reached the table.

Henry talked steadily for the next few minutes, explaining to Dylan exactly how they would use the article, confirming that his picture would be on the front page of the magazine, assuring him that the interview would double the magazine's normal sales. It was nothing less than the truth, but Keely had heard Henry give his spiel dozens of times. He was overflowing with patently false sincerity.

After the waitress had poured Keely a cup of coffee, Dylan turned toward her. He leaned back in his chair with superstar elegance and studied her face, which she kept blank, refusing to let him know he was making her extremely nervous.

"You look vaguely familiar," he said in the dark brown voice she had last heard in a movie theater. "You remind me of someone I used to know. Vaguely."

"You remember her vaguely or I resemble her vaguely?" she asked, her voice sweet enough to choke a grown man.

But not a superstar. Dylan merely smiled and let the question pass. "Henry tells me you're very good at what you do. Somehow I had the impression that Henry preferred voluptuous blondes."

As slurs went, it was a beaut. Very subtle, almost elusive. If she hadn't been so angry, she would have applauded. Because subtle or not, it was an insult. He was implying Henry employed her because she was female, and maybe because she was a willing female.

So it's going to be war, she thought, gritting

her teeth. She was ready for him. She wanted to do something violent, something painful, that would show him exactly how ready she was. He had no right to make assumptions about her. Her eyes narrowed, but before she could even begin to retaliate, Henry spoke.

"She could be bald, for all I care," Henry said, his tone revealing the insult missed him completely. "As long as her brain works."

"And I'll just bet it does," Dylan said.

Somehow the so-innocent words were even more insulting than his last statement. Keely wouldn't let it get to her. She would forget retaliation. She would be polite and professional. If Dylan wanted to play adolescent games, that was no skin off her nose. Keely was above that kind of behavior.

When a man at the next table sneezed, Henry turned toward the explosive noise. Taking advantage of the distraction, Keely raised one hand and gave Dylan a digital, and thoroughly professional, opinion of his last comment. *So there*, she told him silently.

He sucked in a sharp breath and half rose from his seat. Keely watched him, her eyes wide, assuming he was going to throttle her, but seconds later Henry turned back to the table. Dylan shifted in his seat slightly, as though trying to get more comfortable.

Keely sent him a sweet smile, then turned to Henry. "You didn't tell me how long— Ow!" she gasped suddenly.

Henry frowned. "What the hell's wrong now?"

She shook her head. "Just a cramp in my foot . . . a large cramp."

"I hate it when it does that," Dylan said, his voice sympathetic.

Keely was wondering how she could accidentally spill her coffee on Dylan when Henry pushed away from the table and stood up. "Okay, I guess that about does it. I'll leave you two to get on with it."

Keely's head jerked toward her boss. "Aren't you staying for breakfast?"

"I ate at home," Henry said. "I just wanted to stop by to make the introductions." He glanced at Dylan. "Keely has her own way of doing things. I promise this won't be like any interview you've ever had."

"You can say that again," Dylan muttered as Henry walked away.

She exhaled slowly, then swung her head toward Dylan, her eyes narrowed. "Really sophisticated, Dylan. Stepping on my toe." She snorted in contempt. "It's exactly what I should have expected from you. Pettiness and irresponsible behavior."

"*Me?*" he exploded. "You're accusing *me* of irresponsible behavior? What about you? Who flipped whom off? And why in hell are you here? Why didn't you disqualify yourself?"

"This is not a track meet. Why should I bow out?" she countered. "Everyone wants to know What Mr. Hot Pants Tate is doing. It'll make a damn good story. Why shouldn't I be the one to write it?"

"Why shouldn't I be the one to shake you till your teeth rattle?"

Through clenched teeth she said, "Maybe because you value your testicles."

They had both leaned steadily forward until their noses were almost touching. "Charming," he said acidly. "You haven't changed. You're still a pig-headed, outrageous *brat*."

"And you're still a sulking, bad-tempered, bad-mannered yahoo."

"Listen, you imitation of a woman—" He reached out and grabbed her shoulder, pulling her closer.

And that was all it took. In that instant Keely forgot the interview and her job. She forgot the café and the people in it. She forgot everything. With a soft, breathy moan she leaned toward him, aware of nothing except the overpowering need to touch him.

"Son of a bitch," he whispered hoarsely, dropping her arm as he turned away from her.

He clenched his fists and repeated the words over and over again. Finally he took off his sunglasses and threw them down on the table before turning his head toward her. "I was crazy to think this would work. I think it would be better for everyone if we forget the whole thing."

Keely had already opened her mouth to agree with him wholeheartedly when she remembered her job and Henry. "Better for everyone?" she asked, shaking her head. "I don't think so. Typical behavior, Dylan. You can forget your friend Henry; you can forget my job. Just make sure Mr. Dylan Ain't-He-Wonderful Tate is comfortable. You've always tried to screw things up for me. I don't know why I should have expected it to be any different now. You can walk away and forget it, but what about me? What about my job?"

She paused, biting her lip to force calm into her voice. "Look, just before we split, you told me that it would never work for us because we are opposites. Little Miss Muffet and the Street Rat, remember? Are you going to let Miss Muffet outtough you?"

He took several deep breaths, then his lips twisted in a crooked, rueful smile. "You've put on weight, kid." His voice was reluctantly admiring. "Your punches didn't used to sting quite so much."

She laughed. "Not quite so bright-and-shiny new, am I?"

"Not quite." He met her eyes. "So. How's life been treating you, Keely?"

She took a sip of coffee. "Not too bad. I like my job. I like my life. How about you?"

He shrugged in a casual movement. "I can't complain."

"I should hope not." She smiled stiffly. "Women dream about you, and men do their damnedest to copy you. What's not to like?"

He grinned. "Like I said, I can't complain. I get better tables in restaurants now."

It was a Dylan kind of statement. She had never been able to discover whether his attitude was real or simply a wall he hid behind.

He shot a glance at her. "You cut your hair."

"Waist-length hair isn't practical. Too unmanageable." She grimaced. "It's still unmanageable, but there's not as much of it to fight now."

He was silent for a moment. "The fact that I asked you never to cut it probably had nothing to do with your decision."

The words were softly spoken, but Keely saw red. "What makes you think anything you ever said could have influenced me one way or the other?" she asked, spitting the words at him.

"Yeah, what makes me think that?" His voice was hard, cynical. "Nothing I wanted ever meant a damn thing to you. A couple of years of fun and games, then toss the old man out on his ear."

She coughed, choking on furious indignation. "I tossed you out? You must be getting senile. You ran so fast you made my head spin. Magic Dylan—now you see him, now you don't. I came home one day and you were gone. Just as if you'd never been there. You didn't leave anything behind except your teeth marks on—"

She broke off abruptly, glancing away from him as hot color flooded her face.

"My teeth marks on the inside of your thigh," he finished huskily. "At least that part of our relationship was always good. It was more powerful than we wanted, there at the end, wasn't it? Even when we were throwing furniture at each other, it was there." He leaned closer, examining her face. "Do you still make those throaty little sounds when you make love, Keely? Do you still—"

"Shut up!" She jumped to her feet, almost knocking the chair over in the process. "You were right. This was a mistake. A stupid, stupid mistake."

Then she walked away from the table and out of the café.

Dylan leaned back in his chair and watched her until the door closed behind her. He felt an uncontrollable surge of fury sweep over him. He wanted to kick something, throw something. He wanted to make Keely pay.

Dylan hadn't felt this particular kind of anger in five years. Not since the last time he had seen her.

Little Miss Muffet and the Street Rat, he thought with a harsh laugh. That was the label he had pinned on the two of them the day after they had met.

Before they had said good-bye, the night of the party, they had agreed to meet the next morning at a park on the lake near the Ellis home. Dylan had arrived early and leaned against his car as he waited.

The bluebonnets were just beginning to bloom. Everything looked cleaner and brighter than it had the day before. The sky looked bluer, the grass greener. He tried then to work up some healthy skepticism for the way he was feeling, but it was no use. He felt wonderful, and the wonderful wouldn't go away.

The night before had been mind-blowing. He had been attracted to Keely even before he touched her. He had liked the way her mind worked, the way she laughed at herself and at the rest of the world. Affectionate rather than mocking laughter.

Then he had touched her and had gone into immediate sensory overload. He had wanted her last night. He had wanted her desperately. That in itself was unique. It didn't happen that way for Dylan. After he had gotten over the idealism of his teenage years, after the idealism had been burned out of him, he had looked at women with a desire for the outside, for a particular body. With Keely it was different. He wanted the body and the brain and the heart. With Keely he wanted the whole woman.

Just then he heard her call him and glanced up as she ran toward him. "Am I late?" she asked in a breathless rush.

"No, I was early. I wanted to check out the bluebonnets."

She cocked her head to one side, studying him. "You don't look like a bluebonnet man."

"Lord, I hope not."

He took her arm and began to walk along the grassy bank. At first they had just walked, happy to be near each other, then the questions began. Each was eager to learn all about the other. There was a matching need in them to know about the time before. The time before time began for them as a twosome.

Dylan didn't like talking about his past. It wasn't something he did often, at least not when he was sober, but with Keely he found he needed to share as much as she needed to know.

He told her about his mother's death when he was nine and about his father, a man who didn't know how to care. When Dylan's mother died, there was no one around to pull some humanity from Barry Tate; there was no one to provide a connection between father and son. For years after his mother's death Dylan and his father rarely saw each other, and when they did, they had nothing to say to each other. Barry Tate didn't know or care how his son spent his time. He only wanted to be left alone.

"Sometimes he brought women home," Dylan said, smiling at the memory. "We had a signal. If the porch light was on, that meant he had company and I was to make myself scarce." He laughed suddenly. "The only catch was, more often than not he would forget about the light and just go to bed after the woman left."

"You mean you had to stay out all night?"

"It wasn't that bad. He usually remembered in cold weather. In the summer I didn't mind staying out. There was lots of action on the streets. Until about two in the morning. It would get a little lonely after that." He grinned. "At least until I found Joe's place."

"What was Joe's place?"

"It was a little club in south Dallas. They tore it down several years ago, but back then it was a jumping joint. It stayed open all night. Even after the customers left, the musicians would stay and play. Because they loved the music. They lived for the music." He glanced at her. "That's where I developed a taste for the blues. And that's where I learned to play the sax. I also learned to play the guitar, the piano, and the harmonica, but sax suited me best."

He sighed. "I miss those guys." Glancing at her, he smiled ruefully. "It must sound strange to someone who grew up in a little white frame house in Tomball, Texas. I can almost set the scene. Your house had green shutters, your mother made brownies and braided your hair, and your father called you Princess and let you light his pipe."

"The shutters were yellow, Mamma's specialty was chocolate-chip cookies, and Daddy smoked cigars. But only in the backyard. Mama wouldn't let him in the house with them. And he called me Dumpling." She smiled apologetically. "I was pudgy until I was twelve."

"Close enough. We make a swell pair—Little Miss Muffet and the Street Rat. I was right last night," he said, smiling wryly. "We're wrong for each other."

She nodded. "Totally wrong."

He turned her, drawing her into his arms. They kissed as though there were a hidden agenda, and ecstasy was next on the list.

"Now that we've got that settled," he said against her lips, "can I see you tonight? And tomorrow? And the day after that?"

"Yes, yes, and yes."

Now, in the not-so-bright present, Dylan pushed his chair back and stood up, feeling wrung out by memories. He hadn't let himself think of that time, the beginning, for a long while. Keely had been open and honest and so damned loving. But so damned young. Twenty to his thirty-two. He should have been stronger. He was the mature one. He was the one with experience. He should have stopped it before it began.

But he hadn't. He couldn't. The minute he touched her in the dark, it had gone beyond his control, before he had even seen what she looked like. Something in her had reached something in him, something deep and hidden and vulnerable. She fed a need he hadn't known existed.

From the distance of five years Dylan could say their love affair had been a mistake. They were bad for each other. He had hurt her, hurt her bad, and he had been badly hurt in return, worse than he had ever been hurt. But even knowing what he knew now, even knowing the way it had ended, he wouldn't have been able to stop it from happening. Nothing could have stopped it. All of it, the love, the passion, the anger, and the pain, had been inevitable. All threads in a tapestry.

His lips twisted in a wry smile. It was useless to sit around regretting the past, wishing it could be changed. None of the threads could be unraveled. He could only hang on and see what new threads would be added to what was already there. And maybe someday he would be able to detect a design.

" 'All the emotion is absolutely, positively gone.' " Celeste raised a heavy eyebrow at Keely. "That is what you said, isn't it?"

The two women were in Keely's apartment. A pizza, still in the box, was on the coffee table in front of Celeste, who sat on the couch, a large slice of pizza in one hand, a diet drink in the other.

Keely stopped pacing the boundaries of her small living room long enough to glare at her friend. "All right, so I made a slight miscalculation. There's no need for *either* of us to make a big production out of it."

Celeste studied Keely's face for a moment, then said, "How did you feel when you found out?"

"When I found out what?"

"You said he was Dylan the superstar and you didn't know him. You said you didn't feel anything for him. Then, the second you see him again, you get mad as hell at him. You don't get mad easily. So he still affects you. How did that feel?"

Keely frowned. She didn't want to answer the question. It made her uncomfortable, because beneath the anger there had been tremendous relief. Dylan was still Dylan. And there had been exhilaration. She hadn't felt so alive in five years.

She shook her head briskly and began to pace again. "None of that matters. I've got to put this in perspective. I'm a journalist. He's a subject. He's a man people want to read about."

"He's Dylan Tate, superstar," Celeste contributed.

"That's right. He's Dylan Tate, superstar."

"He's nothing to you anymore," Celeste said.

"Exactly! He's nothing to me anymore."

"And you want his body like crazy."

"And I—" Keely broke off when she realized what Celeste had said. Closing her eyes, she whispered, "And I want him so bad I can taste him." She shook her head wildly. "But I can't let that affect me. I'm a professional. I've got to start acting like one."

"And you still say you wouldn't go back?" Celeste asked. "You wouldn't try it again with him?"

"No," she said softly, then more emphatically, "No, I wouldn't go back. We had a love affair orchestrated by Spike Jones. I want . . . I *need* Mantovani."

This wasn't the first time since they had split that Dylan had taken up all Keely's thoughts, all her emotions. It had happened all too often in the months after they split. And once, as she had sat in a darkened theater, she had felt ready to scream in frustrated need. She had heard his voice and the music he had played, and it had been sheer hell, but she had survived. And she could survive this.

She shouldn't have run from him this morning, she told herself. Running away wasn't her style. She should have faced the problem squarely and dealt with it.

"I can do this," she said aloud.

"Of course you can." Celeste picked up another piece of pizza. "Just call him and grovel. Tell him it was indigestion or PMS and ask if you can start again."

Keely didn't think much of the idea. She was imagining the gloating enjoyment she would hear in Dylan's voice when the phone rang, and suddenly she heard Dylan's voice, minus the gloating enjoyment.

"Dylan?" she said, swallowing in confusion.

"Oh my gosh!" Celeste squealed, almost knocking Keely over as she tried to get closer to the telephone. "Oh my gosh, is it really *him*?"

"Just a second," Keely said into the receiver. Drawing her head back, she stared at Celeste and pointed firmly at the couch. When her friend was a safe distance away, Keely cleared her throat and began again. "Okay, Dylan, what can I do for you?"

"That's a loaded question, but I'll ignore it. And as a matter of fact, I'm calling because I want to do something for you."

"What a novel idea," she said, her voice sweetly surprised. "They say that change is good for the soul."

"Do you want to hear this, or do you want to take potshots?"

She considered the question, then shook her head and said, "I'm listening."

"I talked to Henry about an hour ago. He gave me your phone number."

"And why did you need my number?" She couldn't quite keep the suspicion out of her voice.

"If you'll stop interrupting, I'll tell you," he said impatiently. "I called him to tell him the interview is off, but I didn't get the chance. He started thanking me for cooperating."

Keely smiled. She knew that when gushing was necessary, Henry could gush with the best of them. "I bet that made you feel like a pig. An uncooperative pig."

"Keely?"

"Yes?"

"Shut up." His voice was soft but emphatic. "Henry's counting on the interview." He paused, and she heard him draw in a slow breath. "We overreacted. It's pretty obvious we were both hoping the same thing. We were hoping this . . . this thing between us would stay dead and buried. Well, we should have known nothing is ever that easy. But we can't let it matter. We'll simply have to work around it. We'll have to avoid situations where it could spring up at us."

Was he suggesting they meet in a deep freeze? she wondered, but aloud she said, "I've been doing some thinking too. I don't like making concessions to an . . . an obsession. I want to be in control rather than being controlled. We've admitted the attraction is still there. It's out in the open now. And you're right. Since we're aware of the pitfalls, we can simply avoid them. We can handle it."

"Of course we can."

She wasn't positive, but she thought she heard amusement in his voice. It stiffened her backbone. "I'm used to difficult situations. Look, how much time can you give me?" she asked briskly. "Henry explained that I don't just sit down and tape a couple of conversations, right?"

"He said you spend as much time as you can with the people you interview."

"That's right. I've taken as much as two months with a single subject. I'm sure we won't need that much time, but I'll follow your schedule. Why don't you look at your calendar, then get back to me tomorrow to let me know when we can start?"

When she finished speaking, there was silence from his end. Licking dry lips, Keely was suddenly afraid she had been too forceful, too abrupt. The discretion and tolerance for which she was known seemed to be woefully lacking tonight.

She glanced frantically at Celeste, who rolled her eyes and moved her index finger quickly across her throat in a silent assessment of Keely's performance.

At last Dylan spoke. "Okay, I'll call you tomorrow," he said, then hung up.

When she put down the telephone, Keely's hand was shaking. She wasn't sure whether she had won or not. And if she had won, what exactly had she won?

It would be all right, she told herself. Talking to him, seeing him, would get easier. It had to. It certainly couldn't get harder.

Four

Keely paused just inside the entrance to the mall. The ice rink was on her left. Since it was Monday and school was in session, there weren't many skaters, mostly mothers and small children.

Dylan had said he would be waiting for her on the bridge over the rink. She took the escalator to the next level and glanced around. He was there, standing in the middle of the walkway, leaning casually on the rail as he watched the skaters below him.

She began to move toward him, then did an abrupt U-turn and walked to stand in front of a store window. All the moisture in her mouth had suddenly migrated to her hands, and her heart was playing hopscotch.

"Stupid, stupid, stupid," she muttered to herself in frustration.

Her reactions to Dylan weren't only disturbing, they were damned embarrassing. It wasn't fair that after all that had happened between them, she should still have palpitations at the sight of him. She despised the weakness, but it didn't surprise her. Her lack of strength had been a big part of the problem five years ago. Dylan had needed a strong woman, someone who could help when he fell into the black moods that so often plagued him, and Keely hadn't been strong enough. She had been helpless to understand what drove a man as complex as Dylan.

In the beginning, the moods had seemed nothing more than facets of a personality that was being slowly revealed to her. Every new relationship went through the same period of discovery, she had told herself. And since he would always turn to her again when the moods left, she hadn't worried much about them.

Then, a little over a year after they had begun sharing an apartment, everything had changed. She could pinpoint the very day it happened, the day she realized she was not and could never be the kind of woman he needed.

The memory stood out fresh and clear in her mind. He had just come out of one of his black moods. It had been an exceptionally long one, almost two weeks, and their lovemaking—her welcome home to the loving Dylan—had been frantic and exhausting. She had lain in bed, her heart rate slowly returning to normal, and suddenly she hadn't wanted to let him move away from her. An unexpected, unexplainable fear had gripped her, and she was certain something terrible would happen if she let him out of her arms.

She had been right. Dylan had pulled away from her, his movements gentle but firm. Sitting beside her, he had stared down at her. And she had seen then the withdrawal in his gray eyes. He was purposely distancing himself from her.

Until that moment, Keely hadn't known a live body could feel so cold. She had felt cold and lonely and more afraid than she ever had in her life. She had been too weak, too much of a coward, to ask him what was wrong, to ask him what he needed that she wasn't able to give him. She hadn't wanted to hear him say the words aloud. It would have been too final. She wouldn't have been able to pretend that someday they could work it out.

After that night Dylan had taken more out-of-town club dates, and when he was in Dallas, he began staying out later and later. She might have been young and inexperienced, but she hadn't needed age or experience to know that he was avoiding her, that he simply didn't want to be with her anymore.

When they were together, there were more and more arguments, until the arguments were all they had. They hadn't lost the passion, but it was being spent on anger.

Now, five years later, the memory still had the power to make Keely flinch. The end, the final argument, had been no different from the others. Except that it was final. It was that moment, the moment she realized that she would never be able to give him what he needed, that still had the power to sting. Dylan wasn't an ordinary man. He was the genius that critics had labeled him. He was a special man who needed a special woman to match him.

And, like it or not, Keely told herself, she was as far away from special as they come.

Taking a deep breath, she turned around and walked toward the walkway. When she reached him, Dylan turned to lean his back against the rail, nodding to acknowledge her presence. "How are you, Keely?"

He sounded polite. Too polite, she thought warily. "Fine . . . and you?"

"Fine. You don't mind meeting here?"

"No, it's fine."

"That's . . . fine."

They laughed. It wasn't wholehearted laughter or even comfortable laughter, but it was a start.

Regaining his former position, he said, "Look at that little girl, the one with the pink skirt. She looks like that kid who lived next door to us. What was her name?"

"Winnie." She frowned. "She doesn't look anything like Winnie. Winnie was a horror. She stuck her tongue out at me every time you turned your back."

He chuckled. "You always had a way with kids."

"Normal kids adore me. Winnie was not normal. Winnie was a jealous, vindictive, five-year-old brat. She wanted you all to herself. I think her mother spent evenings coaching her, telling dear Winnie what a wonderful father you would make."

"I don't remember her mother."

"Oh, sure." Keely's voice was openly skeptical. "You don't remember the blonde with the thirty-six D IQ? Every time we went down to do laundry, she just happened to wander in. No one washes clothes in a bikini. I never saw that woman fully clothed."

His eyes widened. "So *that* was Winnie's mother."

"I thought you'd remember. I was surprised you didn't move in with her after you did your disappearing act."

Violent anger flared in his gray eyes, and his features hardened. "When did I ever give you reason to think I would do something like that? There were plenty of willing women at every club we played. When did I *ever* pay that kind of attention to one of them?"

"Three and a half months before you left," she said without hesitation. "She was petite, plump, and had short black hair. When I walked into the club, she was sitting on your lap."

His shook his head, furious incredulity in his eyes. "I don't believe you. I really don't believe you. I explained about that woman." He stiffened suddenly. "You mean you were lying when you said you believed me, when you said you believed it was all an innocent mistake?"

"Yes," she hissed, moving closer to him. "I was lying. I hated her and I hated you. You were laughing with her, laughing at me. And the next night, you didn't come home. You stayed out all night like the alley cat you are, you bastard! Your morals rank right up there with your loyalty."

"You self-righteous, judgmental, backwoods—" He broke off and inhaled slowly, his nostrils still twitching with anger. "This is ridiculous. Maybe we'd do better down on the ice. It'd give us both a chance to—"

"Play roller derby?"

"—work off some tension," he finished tightly. After a moment, he flexed his shoulders, and when he spoke, his voice was calm. "How about it? I haven't skated in years."

She shook her head. "Not today. It's Monday."

"What does Monday have to do with anything?"

She glanced away, avoiding his gaze. "I meant it's too early," she mumbled.

"You said it's Monday."

"What are you doing—recording the minutes? What I meant was that Mondays are always bad days. Everyone knows that. It's a scientific fact that more accidents happen on Monday than any other day of the week."

He stepped around her so he could see her face. "It doesn't have anything to do with Mondays," he said, and there was knowledge in his voice, knowledge and amusement. "You're wearing the wrong panties, aren't you?"

She swung her head away from his dissecting gaze. "Shut up," she said through clenched teeth.

He gave a loud snort of laughter. "I don't believe it. You're not wearing your Monday panties, and you're afraid it will jinx you."

A young man wearing bright yellow shorts paused beside them, his interest well and truly caught. Keely glared at him. "Do you mind?"

Dylan grinned at the man's hasty retreat, then said, "Come on, admit it, Keely."

"Okay, okay. I forgot I hadn't put them in order. I was in a hurry this morning and just grabbed the top pair."

"How do you know the top pair wasn't Monday?"

"Because I checked in the car on the way here." She grimaced. "Thursday, big as life."

"How many wrecks did you cause while you were checking the monogram on your panties?"

She grinned. "The pickup beside me swerved across a couple of lanes, but there was no damage done." When he laughed even harder, Keely sobered. "We're not supposed to be discussing my underwear. I'm supposed to be interviewing you."

He shrugged. "Whatever you say. But let's walk while we do it."

She stole a glance at his face. Earlier, instead of turning her face toward him, he had moved around her so he could see her face without touching her. Now, he kept a slight but noticeable distance between them as they walked. It didn't seem likely, but he was acting as though he was as wary of her as she was of him.

Dylan shoved his hands in the pockets of his slacks so he wouldn't unconsciously take her arm as they walked. Touching her in public was not a good idea.

"Where do you want to start?" he asked.

"Just fill me in on the past five years."

She made it sound simple. How could he tell her about those years? The first few months without her had been a black, empty hell. Even after all this time, he still didn't like to remember those days. Sartre said hell was other people, but he was wrong. Hell was the absence of one particular person. Hell was knowing you could never have the one thing that mattered most.

Dylan had thought then that he would never make it out of that obscenely lonely place. The past had bound him. It was only when he had found the strength to contain the memories that he had been able to fight his way out. As the song said, he had put time in a bottle. The time he had spent with Keely. He had shoved all the memories into a bottle in his mind and had corked it good and tight. Then he had, step by step, started to live again.

But he couldn't tell Keely any of that.

•   •   •

When the silence between them lengthened, Keely frowned. "It wasn't a real tough question," she said, "but if you need something more specific, tell me about moving to New York."

He shrugged. "We were playing at a little club on the East Side. I liked the scene and decided to stay."

"Must you babble on?" she muttered. Then: "Could you fill that out some, add just a teeny bit of background to it? 'He shrugged' is not the kind of stuff people want to read."

"I don't know what you want me to say. I talked to the guys, and we agreed it would be a good move."

There was no need for her to ask who "the guys" were. She knew them well. They were Michael Przhevalski and Joseph Salazar, the other two members of the Dylan Tate Trio. Michael, alias Little Nikita, played keyboard for the trio. He stood 5'6", and although his family had come to the United States when he was five, he insisted on retaining his Russian accent. He said it added a certain something to his overall sexual image.

Joseph Salazar was Sally to his friends. He was tall, bone-thin, and black. He played bass, harmonica, guitar, and drums, among other things. Sally would play a summer squash if he thought he could get an interesting sound from it.

"How are the guys?" she asked, smiling.

"Nikita's engaged."

"You're kidding. That wild and crazy guy?"

"Afraid so. He met a little Georgia peach out in California. She smiled, batted her eyelashes, and Little Nick was a goner."

"And Sally?"

He glanced away from her. "Sally and Tanya split about a year ago."

Keely closed her eyes as a heavy sadness settled over her. She had liked Tanya. They had supported each other when the trio was out of town. But Keely had always known Tanya was dissatisfied, at times even angry. She hated the lifestyle Sally's profession forced on them. She wanted him to have a regular nine-to-five job. It seemed to make no difference that Sally would have withered without his music.

"How is he?" Keely asked softly.

"How the hell do you think he is?" There was anger in Dylan's voice and, unaccountably, accusation. "He got dumped. He's hurting."

Biting her lip, she wondered about what was hidden in his tone. She wanted to challenge him. She wanted to ask why he was trying to pretend she had been the one to end their relationship. Was it more comfortable for him? Did it make him feel self-righteous to pretend he had been dumped?

But she knew she wouldn't ask. Some doors were better left closed. "So you talked to the guys about relocating in New York?" she asked, her voice carefully casual.

After a moment he said, "They liked the idea, so we moved. It worked out okay. There's a pretty strong blues following in Manhattan. We got some good publicity, some good reviews."

"Is that how you got the offer to do *Sligh*?"

"Sort of. A guy came in one night. Rodney Weems. He's a producer, and he had recently agreed to do a film for Prestige Films. Prestige had a reputation for slasher films, but this project was different. It was about a down-and-out country singer living and working in West Texas. Rodney really liked the script, but was worried that people would think it was a rip-off of *Tender Mercies*."

"But they weren't anything alike."

"No, but if you give a one-line description—a Texas country singer down on his luck. See what I mean? Anyway, Rodney was going to be in New York for a few days, so he comes into the club one night. He hears me playing, hears me talk—I'm afraid my Texas accent is a little obvious—and he has a brainstorm. He thought maybe the project would work if he made one little alteration. Change the country singer to a blues saxophonist. The story stays the same, but no one will get it confused with anything else. So he catches me after the late show and lays it out for me. He wanted me to go to Hollywood and do a test. See if I could act. See if the camera 'liked' me. So I'm thinking, What the hell, I haven't been to California in a few years. I might as well go and check it out. So I went out there. I did a screen test. I did lunch with the entire population of southern California— the writer, the director, the whole damn board of directors of the parent company. I played temperamental genius for them all, and before I could say, 'Get real,' I was back in Texas making a movie."

"And the rest, as they say, is history."

"As they say," he said, grinning. "The funny part is, no one had anticipated public reaction to *Sligh*. Everyone—except maybe the writer—thought they were making a nice little low-budget, artsy kind of film. They figured they would be lucky to break even. They made the picture to show the industry that Prestige could put out a quality piece, that they could do more than splatter brains on half a dozen camera lenses." He laughed. "Of course, when *Sligh* started making money, everyone involved had known all along it would be a hit."

"And that Dylan Tate would become a superstar."

"Yeah," he said dryly.

"And then you made the album." She paused. "It was incredible, Dylan. I mean it. It was really superior."

" 'A harmonica, a guitar, and a fat guy who whines'?" he said.

She laughed. "My musical palate has matured since then. I loved the album. Especially 'Hypothetical Heartbreak.' It's totally wild. You're sitting there, really getting into the music, then suddenly the instruments stop, and the three of you sing that stupid refrain." Her voice was filled with genuine enthusiasm. "Everyone loved it. For months those words punctuated every conversation. In the office, on talk shows, even politicians' speeches." She shook her head. "You could meet someone on the street and say, 'How're you doing?' and some smart-ass would give that last off-key bit, 'elderberry wine and sweet potato pie.' "

She hadn't exaggerated the song's success. Everyone *had* loved it. They had loved it because it was campy and funny and even profound in an offbeat way. But Keely was working from a different base than the general public. She would listen to the album and see, in her mind, the three of them, clowning around the way they had done so many times in the past. It always made her laugh. It always made her hurt.

"Glad you liked it," he said. "I guess that about covers the past five years."

It didn't. He had left out all the women. Maybe he thought there wasn't time, she told herself. It would probably take a couple of years to cover all the women.

Keely wasn't going to ask him. She wasn't ready to hear about his sex life. She doubted she would ever be ready.

They stopped in front of a small dress shop and watched as a mime in the window showed how accessories could change an outfit.

"How did you like living in California?" she asked after a moment.

"It was . . . interesting. A little bee-zar for a simple Texas boy."

She snorted. "Sure. As simple as Einstein's Theory of Relativity. Why did you come back?"

He paused, then shrugged. "It was time. According to the statistics, Texans come home more often than the citizens of any other state. Who knows why? What's bred in the bone and all that jazz."

He was being evasive, but Keely wasn't going to press this either. Not now. She had plenty of time.

At that moment, as she stared into the boutique window, it occurred to Keely how she could use this interview. It would give her a chance to do what she had never managed to do in their two years together. She could find out who Dylan Tate was. She could unravel the black moods—what triggered them and what made them go away. She could discover their origin, if they were congenital or the result of some childhood trauma. When she did that, when she had at last succeeded in deciphering the past, maybe the past would finally rest in peace.

"You sure are doing some hard thinking." Dylan's voice broke into her thoughts. "Are you planning all the nasty things you're going to say about me in your article?" he asked.

She laughed softly. The next moment, when she stepped back from the window, she inadvertently did what they had both been trying to avoid since they had met on the walkway. She backed directly into him. The second she felt his hips against hers, she tried to turn around and step forward at the same time. But she moved too quickly and stumbled, making an awkward situation worse.

His hand automatically went to her hip to hold her steady. He could have removed his hand at that point, but he didn't. She felt his fingers spreading across her right buttock. And to her shame, she felt her hips move, pressing her closer.

She jerked her head up, meeting his eyes. Silently she shook her head in a denial that came much too late.

He stared down at her, and after a moment swallowed with difficulty, "If—" He broke off and cleared his throat. "If you'll move your hip, I'll move my hand."

No words would come. She simply continued to stare at him.

"You want to go first?" he asked hoarsely.

She shrugged, giving him a helpless look.

"I'll count to three and we'll move together."

She nodded.

"One . . . two . . . two and a half . . ."

She laughed, drawing in a deep breath as she leaned her head, just for an instant, against his shoulder. Then she moved away from him, thanking him silently for having the strength she lacked.

"I think I have enough for today," she said quietly. "You gave me some good material, and I . . . well, thanks for your cooperation."

"Should we shake hands now?" he asked, his voice dry.

She ignored the sarcasm, just as she ignored his unwavering gaze. "When can we get together again?"

"I'm meeting some guys tomorrow night for a

jam session at Tankersley Inn. Nikita and Sally will be there." He paused. "You can come if you want."

"I'd like that." She glanced around, touched her hair, her purse, then shifted her weight from one foot to the other. "Well, I guess I'll see you tomorrow, Dylan."

"Yeah . . . see you."

As she walked away, a tremor of relief shook through her. The fact that she had survived their first session together gave her confidence for the future. Nothing disastrous was going to happen. She would be able to handle it.

She was not going to be able to handle it.

The lamps in Keely's bedroom were switched off. There was a full moon, and softly muted light slipped through the partially closed drapes, falling across the bed. It was an old bed. The lacy white ironwork reached halfway up the wall. A peach comforter drooped over the side, half on, half off.

Keely lay spread-eagle in the exact center of the bed. She was hot, even though she had switched on the air-conditioning unit earlier, even though she wore nothing more than a pair of bikini panties. The panties were cocoa silk, and on the upper left side the word MONDAY was monogrammed in *café au lait* thread.

She lay unmoving for a long time, then she closed her eyes. Almost immediately she saw, as clear as a movie playing on the inside of her eye-lids, two people and a bed. It wasn't the iron bed. There was no headboard, and the comforter was navy blue. The comforter lay on the floor, in a pile with the pillows and a sheet. There was nothing on the bed except a fitted sheet and two naked bodies.

Keely clenched her fists, but she didn't open her eyes to make the scene disappear. She couldn't. She had discovered—at this very moment—that she had unsuspected voyeuristic tendencies. She wanted to watch them. She hungered to watch these bodies, these tangled arms and legs. She was desperate to see two pairs of hands sliding over smooth flesh. She ached to see the hard, tanned buttocks tense, revealing every muscle, as . . .

"That's *enough*!" she whispered, her body glistening with perspiration as she rolled over and punched her pillow.

She had to deal with this. She had to be rational. It was only natural that seeing him would trigger hidden—carefully hidden—desires. She would simply have to learn to deal with it.

She turned over, lying flat on her back again, her body straight, her hands at her sides. She knew the routine; she had used it often enough. She would start at her toes and relax each part of her body. It would work. She would make it work.

That's right . . . toes relaxed. Now the rest of the feet. Way to go, feet. Come on, calves, stop

*twitching. Do your thing . . . relax. That's right.
Okay, on to the knees.*

But her knees rebelled. Instead of relaxing, they
began sending forbidden messages. She felt his
fingers on the backs of her knees, doing the tick-
ling, stroking thing he always did. And fast behind that sensation came the feel of his teeth on
the inside of her thighs.

Catching her breath, she grabbed the pillow
and pulled it into her arms, covering her face and
chest. Without her consent, her bare breasts began to stir against the percale pillowcase, the movement automatic . . . needful . . . deprived.

Her whimpering moan sounded loud in the dark
room.

In room 811 of the Fairmont Hotel, the light
had been left on in the bathroom, spreading a
discreet white glow into the bedroom. The light
extended across an armchair full of green bed-
spread, but fell short of the four-poster bed. On
the bed were white cotton sheets, extra feather
pillows, and a beige blanket that had been pushed
to the end of the bed. And Dylan.

He lay on the far right of the bed. His hands
were folded beneath his head as he gazed at the
ceiling. He wore nothing except a watch with a
wide brown leather band.

He kept thinking about the moment in the mall
when they had stood staring at each other, the
moment when they had acknowledged, once again,

that it was still there. All the hunger, all the desire. All the memories of love.

Now, closing his eyes, he pulled up a vivid image. He saw her sitting cross-legged on the bed as she combed the tangles from her just-washed hair. She wore silly little panties the color of a sunrise. He couldn't see the monogram. This particular set announced the day right square on her butt. But he knew they were SATURDAY. He knew because he had given the day a quick feel when she had walked by minutes before.

As he watched her, she bent her head and her long hair fell across small, high breasts. She knew he was watching. She pretended she didn't notice, but she knew all right. Her nipples were constricted and hard. Dylan was in awe of her breasts. They were amazingly, incredibly sensitive. He had brought her to fulfillment more than once simply by fondling and biting her breasts.

"What did you say?" he asked abruptly.

She glanced up as he moved closer to the bed. "I didn't say anything."

He sat on the bed and pulled her across his lap. "Not you. Your boobs were talking to me."

She raised one brow. "Oh, yeah? What did the sneaky little devils say?"

"They were asking me a question. A question to which I'm trying to formulate an answer. I could say—" He broke off to roll one nipple between his index finger and thumb. "Or I could say—" Lifting her upper body, he took the other nipple into his mouth, teasing the taut sweetness with his tongue.

She gasped, letting her head drop to his shoulder. "Orator Tate," she whispered, her voice breathless. "You leave William Buckley in the dust."

Seconds later, she pushed him back on the bed and wrapped her arms and legs around him. She did things that only she . . .

Dylan sat up abruptly, dragging his thoughts back to the present, back to the empty hotel room. It had to stop. Now. He wasn't doing himself a bit of good. He was only making it worse.

Pulling the pillow from under his head, he threw it across the room, then lay flat on the bed. There was a yoga exercise that worked for him . . . sometimes. Sometimes he could relax his body so completely, he felt as though he were floating above the bed.

Unfortunately sometimes wasn't this time. The moment his rigid muscles began to lose tension, he felt her above him, her hair brushing against his bare chest, her lips warm on his throat, her thighs moving against his, teasing him, driving him crazy.

In a stiffly uncoordinated movement, he rolled onto his stomach and drew in a harsh, ragged breath. The groan, when it came, seemed to linger over the big, lonely bed.

Keely sat on the side of the bed, rhythmically pounding the mattress with both fists. *Maybe exercise would help.* She could run around the block a couple of times. *And get mugged?* What a stupid idea. It was too late and too dark.

She left off pounding the bed to rub her temples. There was always Jane Fonda and the VCR. *And watch all those peppy, happy people?* Getting mugged would be better. But there had to be something else. *Push-ups?* As soon as the idea occurred to her, she shook her head. Not push-ups. They were too suggestive. She would probably see him beneath her.

Inhaling deeply, she threw back her head in frustration. Maybe she should go find Dylan and break his face.

Now there was an idea she could live with.

Dylan paced the perimeter of the hotel bedroom. What was that girl's name? The one who had been at Tankersley's last night. Coal-black hair, big breasts, and yes-oh-yes eyes. She drank a lot and talked a lot. She said musicians made her sexy.

Grimacing in distaste, he ran unsteady fingers through his already disheveled hair. He had never gone in for groupies, and he would be damned if he would start now. Besides, he didn't want big breasts. He didn't want yes-oh-yes eyes. He wanted small, responsive breasts and go-to-hell eyes. He wanted the only woman who had ever been able to give him what he needed.

•   •   •

Keely faced the back of the shower and let the cold water stream over her back. She turned quickly and gritted her teeth when the icy water hit her breasts and stomach.

Damn you, Dylan. Damn you to hell.

Dylan took a deep breath and stepped into the shower. Every muscle clenched as the cold water hit his overheated body. It was unpleasant, but he didn't turn away. He moved aggressively into it, letting it drench his head and shoulders.

Damn you, Keely. Damn you to hell.

Five

"I think it's sweet that he remembered your panties," Celeste said. "It's even romantic in a peculiar, fetishistic sort of way."

It was late in the evening on Tuesday, the day
after Keely's meeting in the mall with Dylan. Keely
and Celeste had been to their regular Tuesday
night dinner and now sat in Keely's living room,
passing time until Keely left to attend the mid-
night jam session at Tankersley's.

From her reclining position on the couch, Keely
cut her eyes toward Celeste, who sat crosswise in
an armchair. "Fetishistic?" Keely asked. "He didn't
wear them; he just remembered them. And aren't
you the woman who said romantic is a guy who
owns a lawn mower and likes to use it?"

Celeste waved a dismissing hand. "That was during my cynical phase."

"That was a phase? When did it end?"

"Yesterday. Today, I'm a romantic." Celeste tilted her head back. "Today, I'm open to all the possibilities life holds for me. Today, I think the groaner who calls me at three in the morning sounds kind of cute."

"That doesn't sound romantic. That sounds desperate."

"I'm not going to argue semantics." Celeste rubbed her chin. "As a matter of fact, desperate pretty well covers it. My list of things I will absolutely not accept in a prospective husband is getting shorter every day. This week I'm allowing men who give their pickup trucks cute names. Next week I'll allow men called Joe Bob and men whose noses whistle when they breathe."

Keely started to laugh, then changed her mind. Something in Celeste's tone caught her attention. After a moment she said, "You're serious."

Celeste glanced away. "You've had your great love affair," she said, her voice husky. "I know it knocked you for a loop, but would you go back and erase that time? If it were possible, would you change the past so that Dylan had never happened to you?"

Would she? Keely wondered. If it were possible, would she wipe everything out? She wouldn't mind being free of the memory of all those crippling arguments, all the misery and the self-doubt. But that meant she would also have to wipe out the memory of heart-level communication, the memory of a love that was, for a while, more perfect and more satisfying than anything she had encountered before or since.

"No," she said quietly. "I wouldn't erase it."

"Damn right, you wouldn't," Celeste said. "I'm almost thirty, Keely. My feet get colder and colder every night . . . not to mention various other body parts. I'm tired of being alone. I have a God-given talent that's going to waste." When Keely raised both brows in a silent question, Celeste waved one hand. "Not that, although I'm pretty good at that too. I'm talking about being a born nagger. I have no one to browbeat. I need a man to annoy the hell out of."

As Keely studied Celeste, an idea began to take hold. "You're on the verge of allowing dweebs and nose whistlers into the competition"—Keely swung her feet around to sit up on the couch—"which means your requirements have loosened considerably."

"I don't like that look," Celeste said, her voice wary. "What are you plotting?"

Keely grinned. "How about Wayne?"

The brunette choked on a mouthful of air. "I'm not that desp—" She broke off and stared at the ceiling. Seconds later, she sighed heavily. "Bring him with you to dinner next week."

Keely laughed. "Don't sound so depressed. You haven't given him a chance."

"Wayne doesn't deserve a chance. Wayne doesn't deserve a life."

"You think so?" she said, her voice carefully detached. "The way I see it, Wayne's not only a real sweetie, he's also *very* easy to browbeat."

"Sneaky, Keely, real sneaky," Celeste said, laughing. "Okay, I'll give Mr. Entertainment a shot at me." She glanced at her watch. "It's twenty till twelve. Shouldn't you be making a move?"

"I know what time it is," Keely said irritably.

"Well, come on, girl, check your panties and hit the road. The Lord, in that droll way of His, is giving you another chance to make a fool of yourself."

"I knew I could count on you for support. And for your information, I didn't make a fool of myself yesterday . . . or only a little bit," she amended, "and I won't tonight. I probably won't even talk to him. I'll just watch him play and maybe talk to some of the guys."

When Celeste reacted with loud, snorting laughter, Keely threw a cushion at her.

Tankersley Inn was not an inn. It was a small café that specialized in fried catfish, imported beer, and blues. It was owned by a man named not Tankersley but Fred Dockray. Fred said he called it Tankersley Inn to make people ask questions.

At 12:10 the café was empty except for a bartender, seven musicians, and Keely. She sat at a table near the back of the room, where the shadows hid her from view. A young man with frizzy brown hair sang a Muddy Waters tune while the others backed him up on their instruments. Dylan stood near the back of the small stage, the music from his saxophone fusing with the other instruments to make a single sound. Sally shared the microphone with the singer, his harmonica sometimes blending with the voice, sometimes dueling with it. To his left and slightly behind him, Little Nikita stood at the keyboard, his body moving with each note he played.

When the song ended, Sally laughed and pushed the harmonica into his pocket. "You people will have to stumble along without me for a while," he said. "I'm dry."

Before he had even stepped off the stage, the next round of music began. This time Dylan was in the foreground, his sax cradled in his arms as he began to sing.

Keely closed her eyes briefly. She had hoped he wouldn't sing tonight. Dylan's voice was an experience she couldn't describe even to herself. It wasn't smooth, but sweet heaven, it was effective. The sound wasn't picked up only by her ears. It vibrated over her entire body, causing instant, inevitable reactions.

Suddenly a pair of hands came from behind her, covering her eyes. "Guess who?" a voice said.

"Wayne Newton."

"No, but you're close."

"Then it must be a tall, ugly man with the greatest suntan this side of Florida."

The hands were removed. Arms came around her, hugging her, and she heard laughter in her ear.

"What did I tell you about making racist remarks?" Sally said as he sat next to her at the table. He jerked his head toward the stage. "Dylan know you're here?"

"He invited me. Research on the article I'm doing on him," she explained.

Sally turned his head and shouted, "Yo, Nikita! Look over here and see what the wind blew in."

Nikita glanced away from the keyboard, narrowed his eyes, then grabbed his face with both hands. "Keely!" Jumping off the stage, he rushed to the table, lifting her out of the chair with his enthusiastic embrace.

When the small man was also seated at the table, Keely smiled at him. "Dylan tells me you finally got smart." At his puzzled look she added, "The Georgia peach."

"My Sancy?" Nikita said, closing his eyes in ecstasy. "Yes, I love her. You'll always be my adorable one, but Sancy . . . well, you must meet her and judge for yourself. She is in Georgia visiting with her mamma."

Sally looked up from his beer. "If Sancy hears you call Keely your adorable one, she'll have your tongue for breakfast." He grinned at Keely. "The Georgia peach has a temper almost as bad as yours."

"A temper? Me?" Keely asked haughtily, then she laughed. After a moment her smile faded and she said, "Sally . . . Dylan told me about you and Tanya. I'm sorry."

He shrugged. "We all knew it was going to happen. She's happy now. She found herself a CPA, a guy with regular hours, regular paycheck."

Keely felt his unspoken, unacknowledged pain wash over her. She blinked several times, trying to rid her eyes of the sudden tears.

Sally covered her hand with his. "Come on, don't start that stuff. You know what a sap Little Nick is. If you start crying, he will too." He squeezed her hand, then let it go. "So tell us how it's been with you, Keely sweet Keely?"

She shook her head and cleared her throat, shoving the sadness away. "My newspaper job didn't last long. I kept trying to turn all those 'cute' assignments into something important, something that meant something, and they gave me the ax." She laughed. "I don't blame them. I was a little too earnest back then. I free-lanced for a couple of months, then got the job I have now." She shrugged. "All in all, it's been good. I've done some things I'm proud of."

"When did you get modest?" Sally asked, his brows raised in inquiry. "You've done some first-class stuff."

"Yes," Nikita agreed enthusiastically. "That old man who makes windmills, that was beautiful. It moved the heart and made the soul glad. He was a proud man, a good man."

"You read that?" she asked in surprise. "You mean you both knew I work for *Texas Times*?"

If Nikita And Sally knew, she reasoned, then so did Dylan. Which meant he also knew there was a possibility she would do the interview. It was something she needed to think about, but not now, not with two very perceptive men watching her.

"Turnabout's fair play," she said briskly. "Tell me what's been happening. You both look prosperous and a little, dare I say, smug."

"Prosperous, yes," Sally agreed, "but we've got no right to look smug. Dylan did it. Good musicians are a dime a dozen. Little Nikita and I would have made a decent living without him, but we wouldn't have been in demand like we are if Dylan hadn't made *Sligh*. Doing the soundtrack for a hit movie made people sit up and take notice. The LP was just gravy."

Dylan did it. Everyone loved Dylan. Everyone thought Dylan was wonderful. She was surprised to find she resented it. Just a little. Just enough to make her feel ashamed of herself.

Keely glanced away from the two men. There was a question she needed to ask, even if it caused speculation. Staring at her hands, she said, "How has he been? Has he . . . Do those awful moods still hit him?"

When the question brought silence, she glanced up. They were both studying her, their faces equally serious. After a moment Sally said, "Are you asking as a reporter or as a friend?"

It was a fair question. Henry had told her to slice Dylan open and expose the inner workings. That was her job. It was how she made her living. But now that Sally had forced her to consider the issue, Keely knew she would never write anything about Dylan that would hurt him or that would put his vulnerabilities on public display.

She met Nikita's eyes, then Sally's. "As a friend. Always a friend. I just wanted to know." Her lips twitched in a self-mocking smile. "Believe it or not, I worried about him."

"I believe you," Sally said. "Everybody knew how you felt back then, and everybody saw what was happening. It wasn't your fault. It wasn't anyone's fault."

"It was life." Nikita heaved a deep sigh. "Life is always hard on those who love."

Sally drew his head back to stare at his friend. "Have you been reading those crazy Russian books again?"

"You ridicule great literature?"

Keely laughed. "Put the chair down, Niki, and tell me about Dylan."

Nikita shook his head. "He had a bad time . . . right after. For several months we were very worried. He didn't sleep, and he lost weight. And we couldn't help him."

Sally took over. "Then we had to go to New York for that club date. We hoped a change of scene would get his mind off things."

Keely smiled. "And apparently it did. He liked it so well, you all picked up and moved north."

Nikita and Sally, in a conversation that consisted mostly of interruptions, told her about their life in New York, including the night Rodney Weems visited the little club where they were playing.

"Dylan told Weems he wanted the trio to do the score: compose and perform." Sally shook his head.

"Talk about nerve. It's not like he was Tom Cruise or somebody. He was an unknown saxophone player and in no position to make demands, but he told them he wouldn't do it unless we did the music."

"Dylan's never been shy," Keely said dryly.

"Yeah, but if he ticked them off, he would have missed out on the movie altogether," Sally continued. "They could have told him to shove it, but Dylan didn't care. He said if one of us works, we all work. I don't think I would have taken that chance. I don't know that I would have been that loyal."

"I wouldn't," Nikita said. "I would have said, 'It's been wonderful, guys. See you around.' "

"Fast as lightning, without looking back," Sally agreed. "I would have said, 'Nick and Dylan who?' "

Keely laughed. She knew they were lying. They would have done exactly the same. She had spent two years around the three men and knew the kind of loyalty they shared. They were closer and more solid than brothers.

"Tell me about California," she said.

"Ahh, California," Nikita said. "California is different. We tried to shake up the natives, but this is impossible. Walk down the street with two heads on your shoulders, and people will simply say hello twice."

"It was wild," Sally agreed. "And hanging around the show-biz folk was interesting. We spent all our time going from Odessa to Burbank—indoor shots in California, outdoor in Texas—but it was fun."

"Party, party, party," Nikita said, grinning.

"And after the picture was made?" Keely asked.

Nikita rested his forearms on the table. "We thought Dylan would be too busy being a personality to worry about our music. But we were wrong. As soon as the film was finished, we went right to work on new songs."

"But after the movie was released and Dylan got so much public attention," Keely said. "Things must have changed drastically them. Dylan really started playing movie star then."

Nikita laughed. "It was all a joke to him. He would go out and do his imitation of a sex symbol, and then be surprised when everyone bought it. They all thought it was real."

"Including the women," she said, unable to keep the sarcasm from her voice.

"There were a lot of women," Sally agreed. "Why not? They were there. Dylan grew up poor, just like me. He was taught to always clean his plate. He was taught not to waste anything. But after a while he got bored. We could see it coming a long time before it happened. Nothing could hold his attention. He'd even walk out on his own parties. One night he flat-out didn't show up. He had this big do planned. A lot of important people came, but Dylan didn't. The couple who kept his house said he had left an hour before the party was supposed to start. He told them he didn't know where he was going and didn't know when he was coming back."

Nikita picked up the story. "Sally and I got in

the car and began searching. We tried some of the blues clubs, but he was nowhere."

"Then I remembered this place he told me about," Sally said. "It was a lookout, a lover's leap kind of place. He told me he would go there sometimes to try to get it together. So we drove up there, and sure enough, there he was, parked in the middle of all those steaming cars. He was sitting in the backseat of his open convertible, serenading a bunch of people who wouldn't have noticed if Gabriel was standing on their face blowing on Judgment Day."

Sally made a helpless gesture. "So he looks at us and says, 'Friends, you're looking at a man who has it all. I'm the star of the big screen. I've got a best-selling LP under my belt'—by that time *Blues Spoken Here* had already gone gold. Then he says, 'People listen to me like I've really got something to say. They want to be around me. I've got a Jag, a Rolls, and a swimming pool. I've got people who walk around behind me picking up any mess I want to make. I tell you, boys, I've got it all.' " Sally leaned back in the chair. "That's when we knew he was in real trouble. So we took him down off that hill and got him good and drunk."

Nikita picked up the story. "After that he stayed home most of the time. He wrote some music, but he seemed to spend most of his time thinking. Then, one day, he said he was ready to go home. So we all packed up and came back to Dallas."

For a while there was silence at the table, then

Keely said, "You didn't tell me about the black moods."

The two men glanced at each other; then, each in his own way, they avoided looking directly at Keely.

"No, I guess you don't have to say anything," she said quietly. "He hasn't had one since we split, has he? You both told me, way back then, that Dylan didn't have the moods before I met him. He had none before me and none after me." She gave a harsh laugh. "That should tell us something, shouldn't it?"

"Keely," Nikita began, his voice concerned.

"It doesn't mean anything," Sally said.

She shook her head. "I love you both, but facts are facts." She inhaled deeply, then smiled. "Let's talk about something more cheerful. Remember that time Little Nick tried to steal a potted plant from that fried chicken place and that sweet little lady—"

When Dylan walked toward the table, his two friends were laughing, gazing at Keely with the same affection they always had, as though nothing had changed. That was good, he told himself. There was no earthly reason for him to feel the biting jealousy that hit him when he saw them all together.

"Grab a chair," Sally said when Dylan reached the table. "We were talking about that time Keely pushed that guy, he was the manager or something, into the fountain at that swank hotel in San Antonio. And he came up spitting water and curses, threatening to call security, the police, and the CIA. And you just put your arm around Keely and asked if she was through, or if there was maybe somebody else she wanted to push in, like it was something she did on a regular basis."

Dylan grinned, remembering the fury that had radiated from Keely's body that night. The man she pushed into the fountain had been suspicious of Little Nikita's accent and Sally's color and, according to Keely, the way Dylan walked. He had asked questions she found offensive, and she hadn't hesitated in giving him the only answer he deserved.

"We spent the rest of our stay in that fleabag motel," Dylan said, laughing.

"We met some really nice people at that place," Keely said. "Whom we would never have met if I hadn't gotten us all in trouble at the other place."

Nikita stood up. "I have faith in you, adorable one. I knew you tried to drown that man for a purpose much larger than temper. I have to go . . . they're making a terrible sound up there. My genius is desperately needed."

His departure was accompanied by hoots and laughter from the three left at the table; then, seconds later, Sally also stood up. "I'll go get us something to drink. Still drink root beer, Keely?"

She nodded, the movement awkward and mechanical. She wasn't ready to see Dylan alone.

"What did y'all talk about . . . besides old times?" he asked.

"The guys were just filling me in on what's been happening." She smiled. "They told me about some of the wild times you had in Hollywood."

"Hollyweird? They probably made half of it up." Reaching out in an involuntary, instinctive movement, he brushed a strand of hair from her cheek.

Dylan didn't know how it happened or why. He only knew that seconds later they were leaning toward each other. And he knew the kiss, when it came, would be what he had been waiting for. What he had been waiting much too long for.

Then, just as the memory of the taste of her was already on his tongue, mere seconds before they actually touched, Keely pulled the rug out from under him.

She sat up straight, her face pale as she glanced toward the stage. "I'm glad you suggested I come tonight. It's been wonderful seeing Sally and Little Nikita. And listening to you all play again. You still sound terrific."

It was nervous talk. Dylan knew she was trying to break the spell. She was backpedaling furiously, trying to invalidate the emotions that had surged between them moments earlier.

"I'm going to New York in a couple of days," he said quietly.

She swung her head toward him, her big blue eyes startled. He didn't know if she was surprised that he was leaving or simply surprised that he had spoken.

"Business?" she asked.

He nodded. "Something I agreed to do several months ago—a commercial."

Her face changed. Now she was interested, and more than a little amused. "What kind of commercial? Something macho? After-shave lotion? A high-powered sports car?"

"Diet soft drink," he said wryly.

She threw back her head and laughed. He should have been annoyed that she was making fun of him, but he wasn't. He loved hearing her laugh, even when he was the butt of the joke.

"Come with me," he said abruptly.

She choked on her laughter, her face turning almost as red as her hair. "To New York?" she whispered.

"Why not? You could get more material for your article."

She shook her head warily. "I don't think so. New York confuses me."

Dylan stiffened, feeling the rejection hit him square in the stomach. "Crossing the street confuses you," he said, his voice angry and mocking.

Resting her arms on the table, she leaned toward him, hostility in her narrowed eyes. "You're older than I am." Her voice shook with the intensity of her anger. "You may not know some of the current phrases, but I'm sure if you think *real* hard you can figure out what 'up yours' means."

The cut was deliberate. Dylan didn't like her to mention the difference in their ages, and she knew it.

"Why make stupid excuses?" he asked. "If you don't want to work on the damn article, it's no skin off my ass. I'm sure Henry can put someone else on it."

"Why are you trying to pressure me?" She drew her head back, her eyes suddenly suspicious. "Why do you want to get me to New York? What's going on in that tiny little brain of yours? And while I'm asking questions, what was that tender little move a minute ago? You touched me. You—" She broke off and drew in a deep breath, then spoke between clenched teeth. "Listen, sweetie, if you're looking to get your motor overhauled, you've come to the wrong place. You must really be desperate if you think—"

Dylan hit the table with one fist, stopping the words. He swore under his breath, explosive words that poured from him like steam from an overheated kettle. "Talk about paranoid! 'You touched me. You touched me,' " he mimicked viciously. "Judas priest, it was a stupid reflex." He flipped one of her curls with an insolent finger. "This wild stuff is all over the place, as usual. You were practically chewing on it. It was a kindness—like pulling a burr out of a dog's tail—and you act like I was trying to feel you up under the damn table! Are you sure it isn't a case of wishful thinking . . . *sweetie*?"

"A dog's tail? A dog's tail?" she gasped helplessly. "You overgrown, overblown butt head. No wonder you had such a big house in California, you probably need a half-dozen rooms just to hold your ego."

Loud laughter erupted from just behind Keely.

Swinging around, she found Sally, his hands full of their drinks, shaking his head as he laughed at them.

"It sounds just like old times," he said as he placed the drinks on the table.

"It's not anything like old times," Keely grumbled, clenching her fists to keep her voice calm. "You and Nikita have let him get completely out of hand. No sane person could talk to him for more than two minutes without losing his temper."

Dylan picked up his drink. "When we find a sane person, we can check out that theory."

Sally laughed again, glancing at Keely. "So, you coming to New York with us?"

Her head jerked up, and Dylan smiled as he watched the knowledge dawn in her eyes.

"You and Niki are going?" she asked Sally.

"Sure thing. We're technical advisers." Sally grinned. "That means we'll listen and watch and tell them they did a hell of a good job in mixing the music."

"Oh," she said weakly. "It sounds interesting." She took a sip of root beer; then, avoiding Dylan's gaze, she said, "I guess I may as well tag along."

Dylan didn't take his eyes off her. As she talked to Sally, he saw the wariness slowly leave her, and his breathing became less restricted, less desperate.

Earlier, when he had touched her face, Dylan had recognized the look in her eyes as she pulled away from him. Fear. And he had known what she was afraid of. She was afraid they would become involved, again. And that they would have to face the pain, again.

Had it been as bad for her as it had for him? Had she felt as though she had undergone major surgery? As though important parts of her were missing?

For a long time Dylan had fooled himself into thinking he had stopped loving her. He knew better now. He had known for quite a while. He had never stopped loving her, never stopped wanting her. For five years that love had been put on hold, but seeing her had put an end to that. He couldn't hide it from himself any longer. He wanted to share the laughter with her again. He wanted her in his bed, in his arms, in his life.

But if Dylan had learned one thing in his life, it was that there were no guarantees. Keely's fear wasn't without basis. It could all happen again. They could get together again only to realize, once more, that it wouldn't work.

And this time it would probably kill him.

Six

Keely sat in a darkened studio. She hadn't realized there would be so many people involved, but
the set was packed with people and equipment.
The equipment was beyond her understanding,
and so were most of the people. They talked in
some kind of mysterious shorthand that was com-
prehensible only to other members of the club.

Keely the conscientious journalist had made the
decision to come to New York with Dylan. Keely
the woman had regretted it immediately, and the
two sides of her personality had spent several
long nights debating the issue.

It would be an opportunity to gain some in-
sights into Dylan Tate, superstar, the journalist
had pointed out. At the very least Keely would
come back with some interesting photographs.

It would be an opportunity to get kicked in the face, her vulnerable side countered. At the very least, she would come back with some interesting bruises.

When each side had had its say, the debate was a draw. Neither journalist nor singed heart could pass up a chance to be with Dylan.

Keely, Dylan, Sally, and Little Nikita had been in New York for two days, and she hadn't been kicked in the face once. But she had taken pictures, and she had observed Dylan interacting with the people around him. She had watched everyone treat him like royalty, and she had seen Dylan accepting the whole scene as though it were his due.

Sally had told her that Dylan put on an act, but it didn't look like an act to Keely. It looked as if Dylan thought he deserved every bit of fawning that came his way, an attitude that irritated the hell out of her.

Irritation seemed to be a permanent state with Keely. The people irritated her; the city irritated her; but most of all, the commercial irritated her. Earlier in the morning Brad Arbogast, the director, had taken time to explain what the finished product would look like. Although the set didn't look at all realistic, if Keely closed her eyes she could effectively visualize the commercial.

It was going to be a sexy piece, the mood reminiscent of *Sligh*. The camera would first pick up Dylan, his upper body framed by a window, his hip pressed against the sill. He would be wearing tight, faded jeans and a sleeveless army-green undershirt as he played his saxophone. The camera would then slide down to a window two floors below him. A young, beautiful woman would be sitting in the window, wearing shorts almost obscured by a man's large white shirt, the long sleeves rolled up to expose her forearms. She would lean her head back and listen to the music from above as she sipped at a soft drink in a water-beaded can. There would be a dreamy, yearning expression on her face. As the camera focused on her, the music would come closer. Then the camera would pick up Dylan's bare feet on the fire escape slightly above her. In the next second he would appear beside her. She would reach behind her into her apartment to retrieve another soft drink and offer it to him. He would pop the top and take a long swallow while their eyes met and held. The camera would pull away, farther and farther, as music from a lone saxophone floated over Manhattan.

Brad had explained that the long shots and the music would be added later. He explained the mood he wanted to convey. Actually, Brad had explained too damn much. Keely had built an extraordinarily vivid picture of the whole scene. If she had watched the bits and pieces they were actually doing in the studio, it might not have been so bad, but having Brad fill in the details had caused her to discover something unpleasant about herself.

Since she had first seen Dylan again, she had

known that she still wanted him physically. Now she knew that she still felt possessive; that he belonged to her. She had sat all morning watching him work with a beautiful blond actress, and she had wanted to loosen the woman's teeth.

When Brad yelled for everyone to take a break, Dylan walked over to sit in the chair beside Keely.

"Where did Sally and Niki disappear to?" she asked.

"They're with the sound people . . . talking music." He nodded toward the set. "What do you think?"

"I think it'll sell a lot of soft drinks. It has a—"

She paused as a young man brought Dylan a cup of coffee. Dylan took the Styrofoam cup and gave a short nod. Keely studied Dylan's face, trying to read what was in his mind. As though feeling her gaze on him, Dylan glanced at her, raising one brow in inquiry.

"That was a person," she said in exasperation.

"Do what?"

"That was a real, live person who brought your coffee. His name is Hal, he's eighteen years old, and he thinks you're Robert Redford, Jonas Salk, and Abraham Lincoln all rolled into one. You didn't speak to him. You didn't even take the time to say 'Thanks, kid.' All you did was give him the royal nod. The boy is starstruck, so it's understandable that he should think the nod was enough. What blows me away is that you also think it's enough. Sally said you were just playing a game, pretending to be a hotshot movie star, but it's just dawned on me that Sally thinks that because he loves you. He's seeing what he wants to see. I don't think you're playing a game at all. I think you've bought the whole package." She pushed a curl from her forehead with impatient fingers. "Talk about an attitude problem. 'I posture, therefore I am.' "

He stared at her in silence for several seconds, then he said, "Feel better?"

"Yes." She exhaled noisily. "Yes, I do."

"Good. Now I'll tell you a couple of things. Not because I think you deserve an explanation, but because I'm in the mood to explain. First, I have some things on my mind. As a result, I'm not being very communicative today. I admit it, all right? Second, even if I didn't have things on my mind, I wouldn't have acted much different. I probably would have thanked Hal for the coffee, but that's about it. I wouldn't have gotten buddy-buddy with him. A few years ago I would have. Now I can't. Not because I'm different, because *they're* different. None of these people can see past Dylan Almighty Superstar Tate. It throws them off balance if I try to be me. They don't know how to react to it. It may sound like a cop-out, but I'm being kind by living up to their image of me." He gave a harsh laugh. "And you don't buy a bit of it, do you?"

Frowning, she rubbed one temple. "I don't know, Dylan. I just don't know. You're right about one thing—it sounded a lot like a cop-out."

But was it? she wondered. Although the words sounded like an excuse, there had been truth in his voice, in his face. He believed what he was saying. He believed that if he allowed them to see the real Dylan, they would all be disappointed. Was this a conclusion he had reached in Hollywood, or had it begun before that?

"Brad says the sponsor is giving a party tonight," Dylan said abruptly. "He wants me to go to meet the company big shots. What do you think? Want to give it a shot?"

She frowned, her thoughts still held by the puzzle he had presented to her moments earlier. After a moment she nodded. "That's fine. It will give me a chance to meet some more of your fans. And I can always use a picture of you in your party gear."

"Sure, that's why I go to parties."

His sarcastic tone caught her attention. "What's bugging you?" she asked.

"Haven't you ever heard of going to a party just to have fun?"

"Don't be stupid. Of course I go to parties for fun, but this is—"

"Dylan!" Brad approached them, a harried look on his shiny face. "Sharla is sick. She thinks it's the flu, because her boyfriend had it last week. She won't be able to work anymore today." He ran a hand over his smooth brow. "The thing is, it's going to take a couple of days for her to get back on her feet, and—"

"Poor baby," Dylan said. "I thought she was looking a little green. Couldn't we go with what we've got? We must have shot every scene at least three times."

Brad shook his head. "We only shot the scene where she hands you the drink twice, and both times there was something wrong. Once the camera angle was bad, and in the other shot, her hair fell in her face. You're in both scenes. We either wait until Sharla gets well or find someone else and reshoot."

Dylan frowned. "How fast can you find someone else?"

"There were a couple of other actresses in the running. But it's going to take time getting in touch with them. Then, when we find someone, we'll have to run through the whole thing with her. If we're extremely lucky, we could shoot again tomorrow."

Dylan crushed the paper cup between his fingers. "I wanted to get this out of the way today." He glanced at Keely. "You do it."

"Do what?" she asked.

"You can take Sharla's place. You've been watching all morning. You know all the moves."

Brad shifted his feet in embarrassment. "Dylan—" he began.

"Dylan—" Keely said at the same time, shaking her head feebly.

Dylan stood up. "Come on, at least see what she looks like on film. That's all that's necessary. If she looks good, she can handle the rest." He glanced at Keely. "You can handle it." His lips twisted in a slow smile. "Can't you?"

As she sat staring up at him, she suddenly knew what he was trying to do. He was throwing her some kind of challenge. He thought she would object. He thought she would make excuses and back out, and later he would be able to taunt her with her cowardice.

She raised her chin. "Of course I can do it."

Before she could blink twice, Keely was in a dressing room being painted and powdered and pinched. Brad talked rapidly as a hairdresser used some kind of black magic to tame Keely's hair.

Half an hour later, Keely sat in an apartment window, her face glistening with perspiration, her body tense with nerves. The apartment was fake, the window was fake, even the perspiration was fake, but the nerves, regrettably, were real.

Brad had told her they would begin with the shot where she listened to the music from above, and as the music reached her, she caught her breath. It was all pretend, she told herself. Real music wasn't necessary. It would be inserted later. So why did Dylan insist on playing? He said it would help her get into the mood. He said she wouldn't have to pretend to listen because she would really be listening. He said a lot of things, but he hadn't said, not once, that he was going to play the music he had written for her.

I always knew there was music in me, Keely, he had told her several months after they met. *I knew there was music, but I never dreamed— don't laugh when I tell you . . . I never in my wildest dreams thought there was beauty. Until now. You showed me. You helped me find a little hunk of beauty . . . in me. In me, Keely. It just blows me away. This song, this is to tell you . . . well, to thank you for finding it and for showing it to me.*

She wouldn't cry. She refused to cry on film. That memory was supposed to be reserved for late, long, lonely nights. He had no right to pull it up in front of strangers.

But was she all wrong? Maybe he hadn't challenged her earlier, and maybe he wasn't deliberately hurting her with the song now. Maybe he only wanted to get through with the commercial. And maybe he had forgotten the song's origin. Maybe it meant nothing to him.

As the music came closer, the past began to slide away from her, and the rhythm took hold. A throbbing grew in her body; her heart began to beat faster; and her breathing became shallow and labored. Then, suddenly, he was there beside her.

She raised her eyes slowly to his. Automatically, without understanding why she did it, she reached behind her and brought out a can and handed it to him, feeling a little like Eve offering the apple to Adam.

The air around and between them was filled with blatant sexuality, much more than she had detected as an observer. Their eyes met and held. He grasped the can in his hand and stared into her eyes. Neither of them moved. They were held motionless by the surging, swelling sensations that coursed between them. Keely's lips felt swollen, pulsating with feeling as she strained toward him.

From a great distance she heard people laughing and talking. She heard Brad screaming, "People, people!" And still she couldn't look away from Dylan's gray eyes.

After touching her tongue to her tingling lips, she cleared her throat, then whispered, "I don't think we're in Kansas anymore, Toto."

After a moment, Dylan threw back his head and laughed, and the spell was broken. A woman pushed her way between them to mist Keely's face with water in preparation for a new take. Still laughing, Dylan returned to his original position and the torture began again.

They had to do the scene six times. Keely didn't act. She reacted. To Dylan. To the look in his eyes. He pulled the strings, and she did everything he silently commanded her to do.

Afterward, as she changed back into her own clothes, Keely was exhausted. The whole thing had been a mistake. A biggie. *It's all happening again,* she told herself, *and there's nothing I can do to stop it.*

She didn't ever want to see the commercial. She was afraid of what she would see in her own face.

"How many times tonight have I told you how beautiful you look?" Dylan asked.

They were in a penthouse apartment. Most of the world seemed to be sparkling outside the glass walls. The rest of the world was sparkling inside the walls. The large room was filled with people from the soft-drink company, from the ad agency handling the account, and from Brad's film company.

Celeste should have been here, Keely thought. Only a few of the people were cute. The rest, although dissimilar on the outside, seemed to be tied by a single force—ambition. They all moved and talked efficiently, earnestly, and with purpose.

"Are you ignoring me?"

She glanced at Dylan. "Impossible," she said. "No one ignores the star attraction. And to answer your question, you've told me how beautiful I look exactly seven times."

"Not enough. You are beautiful. And that outfit is dynamite."

"This old thing," she said modestly. She wore loose-legged white satin pants that fit smoothly across her hips. With them, she wore a black backless vest. She had pulled her hair back on her neck and held it in place with a large black bow. "This is my Ruby Keeler look. I feel like I should be tap dancing my way across the room." She glanced around the room. "Are we having fun yet?"

He laughed. "Aren't we?"

"Yes, as a matter of fact, we are. I'm glad I came. New Yorkers are a different species. Give this same party in Dallas, and you would see people who were trying to outdress and outshine. Here, they try to outtalk and outwit."

"You're still watching," he murmured. When she raised one brow, he said, "I was just thinking of another party. You're still an observer."

"But you're not still brownnosing."

"No? Why do you think I'm here?"

"Not for that," she said flatly. "You don't have to suck up to anyone. It's the other way around now. And you're watching too."

"Maybe I've learned a little. I can see now that groups of people are made of individuals." He grinned. "But that doesn't mean I can't still make fun of them. See that woman over there, the one whose dress looks like a couple of draped handkerchiefs? She's somebody's girlfriend. Even the way she moves advertises her sexuality. And that woman, the one with the little black dress that cost more than my Jag, she's someone's wife. Those diamonds are advertising how important her husband is. He's the man beside her. The one with the headache."

"And that one"—she nodded toward the third person in the group they were watching—"Miss Dressed for Success, is a working woman. She's going to be running the company someday. Look behind her, about four feet. That guy with the receding hairline is her competition. He doesn't like the way the boss is listening to her. It looks like she's making points, like she's being too clever."

"Receding Hairline is making his move," Dylan said. "He's going to cut her out. He's moving in to outclever her."

Keely shook her head. "It won't work. Basic Black doesn't like him." She paused, then laughed. "Subtle, very subtle. Did you see how Basic Black put her hand on Headache's arm and turned him ever so slightly toward Dressed for Success and ever so slightly away from Receding Hairline?"

"A termite must think the whole world is tough and tasty."

"I beg your pardon?" she said, frowning.

"These people think this"—he waved a hand toward the room at large—"is the world. They don't know, and most don't want to know, that there is another world down there at street level. It's a shame. They're limiting their range of knowledge, their range of emotions." He darted a glance at her. "Let's go find the rest of the world."

One glance from him and Keely felt excitement ripple through her. "Let's do it."

Together they walked, casually, toward the door. Sally looked up from a petite woman in red and grinned at them, giving a thumbs-up. Nikita, on the other side of Sally, waved. Brad had had his back to Keely and Dylan, but he must have seen Sally because he suddenly swung around, his eyes widening in alarm when he saw where they were headed.

"Danger at three o'clock," Keely murmured under her breath.

Dylan glanced around and spotted Brad. Putting his arm around her waist, he began maneuvering her quickly through the guests. One minute later, they were in the foyer. Two minutes later, the elevator doors were closing, shutting out Brad's shouted, "Dylan, wait—"

When they emerged onto the street, Dylan took her hand and they ran. The freedom of the street felt sweet, and they laughed as they ran past uninterested pedestrians.

When they eventually slowed their pace, Keely glanced around. "There's a cab."

"Cab?" He took off his jacket and wrapped it around her. "You can't widen your range from inside a cab. You have to be where the people are. We walk."

And they did. Late into the night they walked and talked and observed. And Keely met the most extraordinary people—a man born in Austria who brought his telescope with him to the newsstand where he worked and talked astronomy to anyone who would listen; a native of Missouri who talked philosophy while he waited for a bus; a woman in a souvenir shop who had been a respected doctor in Thailand and now worked in the garment district because she wasn't licensed to practice in the United States. Keely met a boxer who had fought Muhammad Ali when he was still Cassius Clay, and an artist whose posters, back in the forties, had been in every movie theater in the country.

But the most extraordinary person Keely met was Dylan. A new Dylan. There was no air of noblesse oblige about him; no black mood. None of the people they met on the street knew who he was. They treated him like a nice, interesting man, and he acted like a nice, interesting man. As time passed, she could see him gradually relaxing, as if he thought being a superstar had been a strain.

"Do you think he really fought Ali?" Keely asked.

It was two in the morning and they sat in an all-night coffee shop that couldn't have been more than six feet wide. The only other customer was a woman with iron-gray hair who mumbled as she drank her coffee.

"Why not? Did you see the pride in his face? I figure it doesn't matter whether or not it was the truth as long as it gives him something to be proud of."

"You're a nice man," she said, smiling.

He clasped his heart in a dramatic gesture. "Lord, you must be tired. I didn't hear a drop of acid. What happened to butt head?"

"Yeah, what happened?" she whispered as they walked out of the coffee shop.

Something definitely had happened. It was as though the tension that had kept them both on edge for days had been shelved. It had been put aside for a while so that more important things could take the stage. Tonight, they were almost friends again. Tonight, things were almost right between them.

"You know—" she began.

"I don't think—" he began at the same time.

For some reason, it was funny. It was hilariously funny. Laughing, he pulled her into his arms and held her tightly. When he kissed her, it began in the spirit of fun, of friendship, but what was between them was too strong to simply stay warm. It had to turn hot. It was the nature of the beast.

Keely couldn't think of anything except the way it felt to finally have his lips on hers again, to have his warm tongue back where it belonged. She had survived five years without him, but now she felt she couldn't survive another minute without the feel of his body against hers.

Dylan too seemed to have lost all sense of reality. They stood under a dim streetlight and tried to make two bodies into one.

Long, long minutes later, he reluctantly withdrew his lips. "What are we going to do about this?" he murmured, his voice husky as he rubbed his forehead against hers.

Keely didn't answer for a moment. She couldn't. She was shaking too hard. "We're going to go back to the hotel," she said finally. "We're going to go to bed . . . each to his or her own bed."

He groaned. "I'm sick of cold showers."

She gave a husky laugh. "So am I. But they're better than the alternative."

"Better?"

"Safer," she conceded.

For a moment he looked as though he wanted to argue with her, but he didn't. He simply smiled. "I'm glad you came with me tonight. I had a good time."

She knew the words were more than just a critical opinion. Dylan was asking her a question. She wasn't sure she wanted to answer until she saw the look on his face. It was strangely vulnerable, as though it were important to him to know that she also had had a good time.

"I'm glad I came too," she whispered. "It was wonderful. Really wonderful, Dylan."

He exhaled a slow breath. "Wonderful," he repeated softly, then he took her arm, and together they walked toward the hotel.

Seven

The next morning Keely didn't feel quite so wonderful. The minute she opened her eyes, the full weight of what had happened the night before hit her. She had crossed the line she had sworn she wouldn't cross. And she had done so willingly.

"Willingly?" she mumbled as she brushed her teeth. "How about eagerly? How about, Grab your garters, Grandma, we're going over Niagara with a smile?"

Being in Dylan's arms had felt too good, too right. Just like always. And Keely knew what came next. Five years ago, she'd memorized the script. Another touch, another kiss, and she would be hooked. Keely had no illusions about her ability to withstand Dylan. Too soon, she would come to depend on the touches, the kisses. And she would walk through hell and back to keep them coming.

By the time she joined the three men in the dining room for breakfast, Keely had worked herself into a state of panic. She smiled at everyone, laughing when they laughed, and listened while they talked, contributing a stiff word only when it was absolutely necessary. She just wanted to return to her room as quickly as possible and hide out for the rest of her life.

When Sally and Nikita had finished their breakfasts, they glanced at each other, then stood up. "Would you look at the time?" Sally said. "We're late. Me and Nick made plans to—" He glanced at Little Nick. "What plans did we make, Nikita?"

"We are going out to buy an umbrella," Nikita said immediately.

Sally nodded. "Yeah, we've got to see a man about an umbrella." As they turned away, he punched Nikita in the arm. "An umbrella?" he said in disgust.

The silence between the two remaining at the table drew out until finally Dylan threw his napkin on the table with unnecessary force. "I wanted to finish the commercial yesterday so we'd have time to see a friend of mine today," he said stiffly. "He lives in upstate New York. It's not far, and I thought you might get some good copy. 'Dylan off duty' kind of stuff."

"That sounds interesting." She kept her voice noncommittal.

"That's what I thought until the Great Stone

Face came down to breakfast. Obviously last night disagreed with you." He sounded strange. Hurt more than angry. "Maybe you'd rather go home, forget seeing Cody. Maybe you'd be more comfortable if we leave now."

"I don't know what you're talking about."

"Oh, yes, you do. You know exactly what I'm talking about." Anger had taken over now, and his eyes blazed. "Last night we kissed. Big damn deal. Good grief, Keely, it was a kiss. You're acting like I got you drunk and took you to a humpin' hoedown and now all the dirty details are coming back to haunt you." Through tight lips he said, "It was a *kiss*, for heaven's sake."

Keely felt the heat flood her face, the heat of anger and embarrassment. "Will you kindly lower your voice? People can hear you. And you're way off base. I know very well the kiss meant nothing, and I'm not acting any different than I always act after three hours of sleep. Besides that—" She broke off abruptly and drew back her head, her brows raised in inquiry. "Humpin' hoedown? Did you really say humpin' hoedown?"

He grinned. "That's what Sally and Nick called some of the parties we went to in California."

She leaned closer, her interest well and truly caught. "You mean they really have parties like that out there? I thought that was nothing but a combination of rumor and wishful thinking."

"Well, it's not a requirement for living there— like some people think—but sure, you can find some wild parties in Hollywood," he said. "You can also find them in New York, Dallas, and Boise. If you're looking for them."

"And you were looking? You went to them? Did you—" She broke off and shook her head emphatically. "No, never mind, I don't think I want to know."

"I didn't," he said, his voice dry. "We stumbled across a few, but we never went looking. Now can we get back to the subject? Do you want to take the next plane home to Dallas, or do you want to go see Cody?"

She stared at her orange juice. This could be another challenge. She had accepted his last one, and she hadn't fared too well. But seeing a friend sounded innocent enough, she told herself. And the people around him were usually more informative than Dylan himself. *Dylan off duty.* It would make good reading. She exhaled slowly. And the fact was, he was right. It was only a kiss.

Only a kiss? she thought wryly. That simple little kiss had knocked the ground right out from under her feet. In the early hours of the morning that simple little kiss had tormented her.

She couldn't let it happen again, but she couldn't let it throw her either. In order to complete the article, she would have to see him a lot. And it didn't really make any difference whether she saw him in Dallas, in upstate New York, or in the Arctic Circle. Wherever he was, Dylan was Dylan.

"Okay," she said, laying her napkin on her plate, "let's go see your friend Cody."

It was her imagination, she told herself later. He

hadn't really looked relieved. His gray eyes hadn't really glowed with happiness. With triumph?

Dylan rented a car and, like lemmings rushing to the sea, they joined the massive rush to leave the city. Much more quickly than she had thought possible, they entered a different, less frenetic world.

This was a New York she had never seen. In Dallas, the daffodils had come and gone, but here the countryside was just letting go of winter. Tender yellow-green shoots were only now beginning to break through the frozen ground.

Shortly after noon, they stopped for lunch at a little country inn where the food was good and plentiful, if a little bland for their Texas taste buds.

"Exactly who is this Cody?" Keely asked after the waitress had refilled their coffee mugs. "I don't think I've ever heard you mention him. Have you known him long? Did you meet him while you were living here?"

He shook his head. "No, I met him in New Orleans about four years ago. We were there for a two-week engagement. One night, after we finished up, we all went out exploring the, shall we say, less respectable areas of the city."

"Shall we say dives?"

He laughed. "Right. We found this little club that was so rough, it was almost campy. The comedian onstage was a female impersonator, and he was funny only because he was so bad. So we're sitting there listening to this godawful comic, and a drunk at a table across the room keeps interrupting this guy's routine. The comedian was getting really steamed, but everybody else loved it. The drunk was a lot funnier than the guy onstage. Anyway, this kept happening until finally this humongous bouncer—the kind who has a little skin showing through the tattoos and hair on his arms—grabbed the drunk and tried to throw him out of the place. Well, some of the other patrons took exception, and a few of them took exception with their fists. In seconds it was all-out war. People were throwing bottles and ashtrays and chairs, some of them were throwing other people. Nikita was trying to join in, and Sally was trying to convince him that maybe that wasn't such a good idea. I'm sitting there laughing at them when I felt a hand on my knee."

He laughed. "That made me a little nervous, because my knees were still under the table. But so was Cody. He was on all fours, looking like he couldn't figure out what the hell was happening. I yelled at the guys, and we hustled Cody out. We were going to take him home, but he couldn't remember where he lived."

"He forgot his address?"

Dylan laughed again. "That's right, but it wouldn't have done us any good if he had remembered, because he had also forgotten that he didn't live in New Orleans. It was his first trip there, and even when he sobered up, he couldn't remember the name of his hotel. Anyway, we took him back to our suite, and he passed out on the couch. The next morning he told us he was an artist in town for an exhibition of his work."

He shrugged. "We all got along pretty well, so we spent the next few nights bar-hopping. He was a riot . . . especially when he was drunk, which was most of the time. At first we didn't think much about his drinking, but after a while it was obvious he had a real problem."

"He's an alcoholic?"

He nodded. "We figured it out before Cody did. And when we told him, he didn't want to believe it. It took him another year to admit that he was sick, really sick."

"Did he get help?"

"Eventually. That took another six months. At first he kept saying he could handle it by himself." Dylan paused, the bad memories showing on his face. "After he started going to AA, he was supposed to call a support buddy when things got bad, but he usually ended up calling me or Little Nick or Sally . . . usually at two in the morning."

"And you didn't mind?"

"He was a friend." He shrugged. "Booze was ruining him. It had already ruined his marriage, and it was beginning to mess up his career, mess up his talent. If listening helped keep him together, then I didn't figure it would hurt me to listen."

He was making light of it, but Keely knew he had been a real friend to Cody. "Do you see him often?" she asked.

"We saw a lot of him when we were in New York.

After that, the four of us would get together to help Cody celebrate another year of being sober." He grimaced.

"What?" she said, smiling as she examined his face. "What was that look for? You look like you just swallowed a bug."

"Cody's celebrations are not the champagne-and-caviar kind of thing."

"You wouldn't really expect a reformed alcoholic to serve champagne?"

"No," he agreed, his voice dry, "but Cokes and potato chips would be nice. Hell, peanut-butter sandwiches would be better than what he serves. We play poker all night, and the only thing he puts out is root beer and Gummy Bears. By the end of the night, we're all freaking out on sugar."

She grinned. "Root beer and Gummy Bears? I think I'm going to like this guy."

"Somehow I thought you would," he said.

"Is he a good artist?"

He considered the question for a moment. "I think he's good . . . really good. But when we get there, I'll show you some of his stuff and let you judge for yourself."

Two hours later, when Dylan stopped the car in front of an enormous old farmhouse, judging art was way down on Keely's list.

She stepped slowly from the car and looked around. It didn't feel anything like the farms in Texas. Farms in Texas simply oozed neighborly welcome. This place oozed something entirely different. She told herself if clouds hadn't unexpectedly moved in to cover the sun, the house probably would have seemed more cheerful. If there hadn't been quite so many trees, the word "foreboding" probably wouldn't have kept popping into her mind.

Dylan was already on the front porch, ringing the doorbell. When no one answered, he said, "He's probably working. He likes to wander around in the woods looking for things to sketch."

She glanced again at the woods surrounding the house. "He's got a lot of room to wander. There sure are a lot of trees." She paused, biting her lip. "Dylan, have you ever read *The Turn of the Screw*?"

He made a choking sound, then started laughing, and every time he looked at her, he laughed harder, leaning his shoulder against the door as he shook all over.

"Shut up," she said irritably, moving to join him on the porch. "I can't help it. It feels spooky."

"As a matter of fact"—he threw a comforting arm around her shoulders—"the first time I saw this place, I thought of Stephen King. But I'm a city type. I thought you would feel right at home. Or didn't they have any farms in Tomball?"

"There are farms and there are farms. My kind of farms are big, open places where you plant cotton and watermelons. There's no room here to plant anything. And these trees aren't like the ones back home. These trees look like they're ticked off about something. They look like they'd slap you silly if you looked at them sideways."

Chuckling, he reached above a window and retrieved a key. "Come on inside and look around. You'll see there ain't a haint on the place."

She frowned. "Should we just walk in?"

"That's what the key is for," he said, opening the door. "Cody issues open invitations to all his friends."

The minute she walked through the door, Keely forgot the trees. There was nothing brooding inside the house. The wooden floors of the entry hall and living room were covered with softly faded wool rugs. White, filmy curtains hung at the windows; a delicate landscape hung over the white brick fireplace; an old quilt had been thrown across a pale blue sofa.

"Like it?" Dylan said.

"It's beautiful."

"But utilitarian," he added.

She nodded. "That's part of the beauty. It's not cluttered up with all those fribbly things people put in their houses."

He raised one eyebrow. "Fribbly?"

"Fribbly's a word."

"Not one of mine." He turned toward the stairs. "Cody's studio is in the attic. Why don't we take a look at his stuff while we wait for him to get back?"

Keely felt like a trespasser. She found herself tiptoeing as she followed Dylan up the stairs. But she shoved the feeling aside shortly after they entered the absent Cody's studio. She quickly became involved in the treasure trove of paintings and sketches.

"You're right," she said after a while, "he's good. I like his watercolors best." She picked up a canvas that had been left leaning against the wall. The bold brush strokes and violent blending of color made her flinch. "I wouldn't have known this was by the same artist if I hadn't seen it here. Is he still searching for his own particular voice, or having an identity crisis? There's something Jekyll and Hyde-ish about his work."

"I'm afraid it's a little bit of both," Dylan said, his voice filled with regret. "Cody won't believe he's good. He thinks the only good art is the knock-'em-over-and-stomp-on-'em kind. He tortures himself with imagined defects, then he comes up with something like that." He nodded toward the canvas she still held.

She looked again at the oil painting. "If good means powerful, then it's certainly that. It's also a little scary. It would hold my attention at an exhibit, but I wouldn't feel comfortable having it in my house."

He smiled. "I know what you mean. You stand looking at it, and sooner or later you feel dementia creeping up on you. Deep depression. And anger."

She shivered and replaced the painting. "I think I'll stick with the woodland scenes. They have peace in them."

"They're Cody's real talent, but he thinks they're insignificant simply because they're beautiful. Because they make you feel good when you look at them."

"Bless his heart, he really is weird, isn't he?"

"Maybe a little, but I know where he's coming from. When you stop trying to improve, it's time to pay your hotel bill and check out."

" 'What is called resignation is confirmed desperation,' " she quoted softly, then studied Dylan's face. "You too? You're still trying to improve?"

"Aren't you?"

"Professionally? I guess I am," she admitted. "There's always something in my work that should have been better. Words or thoughts or feelings that elude me. It's frustrating. I feel like I'm just good enough to recognize the fact that I'm not good enough."

He didn't respond for a while. He leaned against the wall and stared at her as though he were trying to read something in her face, something in her mind. "And personally?" he asked, the words quiet but intense.

Glancing away from those gray eyes, she shrugged. "Why mess with perfection?"

He laughed softly, then his laughter faded, and there was only silence. With a rush that almost knocked her off her feet, awareness crowded into the small studio. And right behind awareness came the memories. But they weren't memories of five years ago. They were memories of the night before. Memories of something begun. Something that asked—no, demanded—to be fulfilled.

The air in the room changed. Even the light,

smells, and sounds changed. There were invisible arrows pointing to the man who stood only three feet away from her. Here it is, the arrows said. Here is your desire. Here is the only thing in the world that will make you complete.

"Keely?"

He spoke from directly behind her, and she caught her breath. "Yes?"

"Do you want to go downstairs and play checkers until Cody gets back?"

No! I want you to hold me. I want you to do those things you do to me. I want you to make love to me without stopping for the next fifty or sixty years. I want you to make all the hurt, all the need, go away.

She cleared her throat. "That sounds great," she said without turning to look at him.

"Dylan, dammit, you cheated again."

He sat on the couch, bent over the coffee table. A checkerboard had been placed in the middle of the table. Keely was cross-legged on the wool rug, across the table from him.

He glanced at her. "I can't cheat again when I didn't cheat in the first place. You're just mad because you can't beat me."

"No one could beat you. Every time I take my eyes off the board, you rearrange the pieces. Stop laughing. I hate checkers. You know I hate checkers. Let's play poker. I can beat you at that."

He snorted in disbelief. "In your dreams," he said, standing to clear away the checkerboard.

She watched him store the set in a cabinet, then frowned. "Dylan, I'm hungry. Where does your friend keep his Gummy Bears?"

"Stay where you are," he said, "and I'll go look in the kitchen and see if I can find some cheese and crackers."

He was gone a long time. Keely wandered around the room, restlessly touching polished wood, an iron candelabra, a fat pottery jar. After that intense moment in the studio, she had kept her mind firmly off the night before. She had also kept it away from how it felt being in his arms again after so many years.

As perceptive as Dylan was, it was a miracle that he hadn't sensed what she was feeling up in the attic. If he had known, if he had touched her, even a slight touch, there was no telling what would have happened. She was glad he hadn't known. She really was.

She spent the next five minutes telling herself how glad she was, but even after five minutes, she didn't quite believe it.

When he finally returned to the living room, she stood at the window. Glancing over her shoulder, she said, "It's getting dark outside. Maybe we should go look for him. Maybe he's had an accident and can't get back to the house."

"Not Cody. Besides, he has a dog—a big, ugly mixed breed. The dog would have come back to the house if Cody was hurt." He set a tray of cheese and crackers on the coffee table and moved to stand beside her at the window. "He probably went into town for the day. Why don't we go back to that motel we passed and get a couple of rooms? If we don't run into Cody tonight, we can come back here tomorrow."

"That sounds good." She grabbed a handful of cheese and crackers from the tray and followed him to the front door. "What kind of steak do they have in upstate New York?"

When they were both settled in the car, Dylan reached for the key and turned it. Until he had turned it three or four times, Keely didn't pay much attention.

Frowning, she sat up straighter. "You're just fooling around, aren't you?" she said hopefully.

He rested his forearms on the steering wheel and turned his head toward her, an apologetic smile twisting his lips. "I'm sorry, Keely."

"Don't say you're sorry," she said, nervously moistening her lips. "Say there's a little trick you learned in the navy that will take care of this in a jiffy."

"I wasn't in the navy . . . and I really am sorry. I'm sorry I wasn't in the navy, and I'm sorry I didn't fool around with cars when I was a kid, and I'm sorry—"

"You're sorry you brought me to an empty, brooding house in a car that's broken?"

"That too."

"I accept your apology," she said briskly. "Now how long will it take to get a mechanic out here?"

"Actually that was the next thing I was sorry for," he said wryly.

"You don't think anyone will come out this late?"

His lips twitched. She wanted to ask him what was so damned funny, but she didn't. She waited.

"Did you notice how old-fashioned everything was in the house?" he asked slowly.

She nodded, still waiting.

"Cody's a little eccentric. When he's out here, he pretends he's living in the nineteenth century. It has something to do with pollution and nuclear war."

"He— No, never mind. I won't say anything. Just get to the punch line."

"The way Cody sees it, no sane person can be at peace in the twentieth century . . . because of nuclear weapons and acid rain and chemical additives in the food. And he says he can't paint if he isn't at peace. Since he can't make those things go away, he pretends they don't exist."

"And?"

"There is no television in the house," he offered meekly.

Keely absentmindedly tugged at her ear as she digested the information. After a moment she glanced at him. "This isn't about having to miss *The Cosby Show*, is it?"

He shook his head. "There's no television, no radio and—" His voice faded. He was laughing outright now.

"And no telephone," she finished for him. "Would you shut up! You probably would have stood around laughing while Chicago burned. This is not laughing time, this is figuring out what the hell we're going to do time." She paused. "How far back was that little town we passed on our way here?"

"Oh, I'd say about fifteen miles. Now can I laugh?"

"You do and I'll slap you. I don't . . . Wait a minute, what about the cheese? That had to be refrigerated. Don't tell me your screwball friend has ice delivered."

"No, there's electricity . . . and a microwave, an electric stove, a refrigerator. . . . He has all kinds of kitchen gadgets, but he says a food processor doesn't talk. It won't bring twentieth-century horrors into his world."

"That's stupid. I should have known you would have a stupid friend." She drew in a deep, bracing breath. "So what you're trying to tell me is that we're stuck here for the night?"

"That's about the size of it."

She opened the door and stepped out. "He'd better have a bathroom. I will not—do you hear me, Dylan Tate?—I will not bathe in a bucket in the kitchen."

There was a bathroom. The tub was an enormous porcelain thing with black claw feet, but there was plenty of hot water, and bubble bath that smelled like winter grass.

Keely bathed while Dylan made dinner. She knew from past experience that he was a terrible cook, but she was too angry to do it herself.

No, she amended silently, it wasn't anger that made her movements awkward and her limbs twitchy. It was fear. She wasn't afraid of Dylan. He seemed to have his emotions totally under control. She was afraid of herself. She didn't have anything under control. She was afraid she would make a fool of herself tonight. She was afraid the need would grow so strong in her, she would break under the strain. She was afraid if he showed one tiny sign that he wanted her, she would go down on her knees in gratitude and relief.

Maybe I'd just better stay locked in here tonight, she told herself in disgust.

But dinner wasn't as bad as she had feared. The food was edible. The hot bath had calmed her, allowing her to hold up her end of the conversation without snapping at him.

Her tranquillity, however, was tested every time she saw the gleam of laughter in his gray eyes. He was laughing at her because the situation frustrated her, but she wasn't the only one who was stuck in the middle of nowhere. He was just as stuck as she was. He was simply too dense to see that.

After they had cleared the dishes, after Dylan had built a fire in the little white fireplace, he took his turn in the bathroom while Keely settled on the sofa, pulling the quilt over her.

When they had first arrived, she had felt like a trespasser as she had walked up a stranger's stairs; now, she sat under that same stranger's quilt, wearing that same stranger's clothes.

Earlier, as she soaked in the tub with bubbles up to her nose, Dylan had knocked on the bathroom door. "Bad news," he had said through the door.

"Save it for next year," she called out. "This year is full up." When he laughed, she sighed. "Okay, lay it on me."

"I found a pajama top you can use. And a bathrobe. I'll hang them here on the doorknob."

"That's the bad news?"

"No, the bad news is, Cody doesn't have a single pair of underwear with the day on them. I'm afraid you'll have to go dayless."

He was gone before the bar of soap hit the door.

Now, snuggling on the sofa, she laughed softly. She wouldn't let Dylan see her laugh. She didn't want him to know she found pleasure in the intimacy of an old joke.

Minutes later, when he walked into the room, she surveyed the jeans and flannel shirt he wore. "You're lucky you and Cody are the same size," she said.

"These are mine. I left them last time I was here." He sat on the floor in front of the fireplace, holding his hands out to the flames. "I love the smell of burning wood. It brings out the stunted Daniel Boone in me."

"Didn't you ever go camping when you were a kid?"

He stared into the fire. "No, afraid not."

Keely watched him for several minutes, studying the shadows that flickered across his face in the firelight. "When I had known you, oh, I guess about a year," she said quietly, "I asked Sally and

Little Nick something about your childhood. I wasn't prying. It was just a casual conversation. You know what they said?"

He glanced at her, a crooked smile twisting his lips. "I can probably guess."

"They said Dylan doesn't talk about the past. They said, Don't ask. It hurts him."

He frowned. "I don't know where they got that idea. It doesn't hurt me. I told you about when I was a kid."

She nodded. "That surprised me. I knew more than they did, and they had known you longer. But when I sat down and put together everything I knew about you, I realized it added up to very little. They were right. You don't talk about the past. Except for that one time the day after we met, never. Everyone has memories, whether they want them or not," she continued, speaking softly. "The smells and sounds and sights of the present pull up smells and sounds and sights of the past. And we usually talk about them. When we were . . . before, when we saw quite a lot of each other, I was always talking about things that happened to me in grade school. About my friends. My parents."

"That's because your parents are still in your life. My mother's dead."

"And your father?"

He shrugged. "We lost touch."

"How can you lose touch with your father?" she asked in genuine confusion. "He's not someone you met at camp. He's your *father*."

"There are fathers and there are fathers." He threw her own words back at her. "That night we met, you said I had seen things and felt things you would never see or feel. Be glad of that, Keely. You're crystal clear, through and through. Untainted. Some experiences muddy the waters of the soul. You, better than anyone else, know what I'm like. You know that I'm not an easy person to be around."

"You mean you're a butt head?"

He laughed. "That's not my past. That's my personality. Some things you have to take the blame for yourself. You can't shove them off on things done to you in the past."

"But things . . . things were done to you?"

"I wasn't a battered child." He exhaled in what sounded like exasperation. "Look, don't hunt for things like that to explain me. I know what I am, and I know—" He broke off abruptly, an expression crossing his face that brought an immediate, piercing pain to her heart.

"You know what, Dylan?" she asked urgently. Whatever he had started to say was important. She was sure it was important, that it was some kind of key. "Tell me. Surely you have happy memories? Before your mother died?"

He shifted his position slightly. "Sometimes the good memories get wiped out by the bad. I can remember, just barely, a time when my mother was always laughing, a time when she looked young and so beautiful. But the other memories are stronger, the times when she looked old, the times when she was unhappy." He shook his head restlessly. "She was *so damned unhappy* and there wasn't a thing I could do about it. I couldn't help her."

Keely bit her lip, shaken by the intensity in his voice. "When someone is ill," she said hesitantly, "their personality changes. I know it must have been hard on you, you were too young to understand. But she wouldn't want you to feel . . . guilty. Or responsible in any way."

She paused, waiting for him to respond, but he didn't. "Was it a long illness, Dylan?"

His bark of grim laughter shocked her. "You might say that. But not the kind you're talking about. She killed herself, Keely. She couldn't think of one damn thing she had to live for, so she climbed into the bathtub and slit her wrists."

Keely gasped and slid to her knees beside him. "I'm sorry," she whispered, tears sliding down her cheeks. "I'm so sorry."

"It was all a long time ago." He shrugged carelessly, but his face looked carved in stone.

"Please don't shut me out," she begged. "I'm sorry it happened, and I'm sorry I made you talk about it." She moistened her dry lips. "I can't explain why, but there's a terrible need in me to know. It's important that I know what's inside you, what drives you."

He turned his head, staring into her eyes. "And you don't know why you have a need to know?" he whispered, his voice husky.

She shook her head slowly, silently.

"Because it never ended. We didn't finish. We shut the thing that was 'us' off in the middle." His lips moved in a sad smile. "It couldn't grow, and it wouldn't die."

When her lips trembled, he reached out to touch them with one gentle finger. "If I kiss you, Keely, will you hit me? Will you freak out and get scared again?"

She couldn't look away from the intensity in his eyes. She wasn't afraid anymore. They had communicated. The questions about him had not been answered, but there was a giant crack in the wall between them now.

"No," she whispered. "I won't freak out."

He moved instantly, pressing his lips against hers in a feather-light touch. The sensation overwhelmed her. It swelled inside her chest, lifting her off the ground. She laughed breathlessly as he jerked her against him, and his lips began to wander hungrily, frantically over her face and neck.

"Sweet heaven, it's been so long," he whispered hoarsely. "I can't get enough, Keely. I can never get enough to make up for all those years."

"I know . . . I know," she murmured as she moved her body against him. "It may be the wrong move. It may get us into all kinds of trouble, but I don't care. Just don't stop. Don't ever stop."

A sound came from deep within his throat, and suddenly they were pulling at each other's clothes. It wasn't graceful. It wasn't sophisticated or rehearsed. It was unthinking, undiluted passion. Nothing mattered except getting closer. Nothing mattered except feeling the warmth that lay beneath their clothes.

When they came together, when she felt him fill her, Keely almost cried out in relief. She wrapped her legs tightly around him and held him close. She wanted to remain like that. She wanted to luxuriate in the feeling of being whole again. But they couldn't stay still for long. Need grew too strong too quickly, and they began to move together, urgently, deeply.

It was only short, sweet minutes later when her body surged upward and she heard him groan, "Yes, Keely, *yes!*"

Even afterward, even when the perspiration had dried on their bodies and the night air had cooled their overheated flesh, even after they had made love again and after Dylan had pulled the quilt over them, even when sleep found them, neither of them moved away from the embrace. As though their lives depended on it, they held on to each other throughout the dark hours of the night.

Eight

It was the first rays of the sun streaming through the sheer curtains, warming Keely's face, that woke her. Seconds later, she jerked her head to the side.

Dylan was there, lying on the floor next to her, the quilt drawn up to his waist but not hiding the fact that beneath it he was naked.

A dozen different emotions exploded inside her. She didn't know which to deal with first. She had to get away from there, away from him, so she could think.

Sliding from under the quilt, she moved quietly out of the room and up the stairs. She pulled on the jumpsuit she had worn the day before, but she left the panties. They were the wrong day, and if there was one thing Keely didn't need at that moment, it was bad luck.

When she left the house, she headed, without hesitation, for the woods. They didn't scare her this morning. This morning they looked like a refuge.

As she walked through the trees, she tried to think objectively about the night before. It didn't take long for her to realize objectivity was impossible. And thinking was impossible. There was no way she could be objective where Dylan was concerned, and every time she tried to think, she felt instead.

Her body had changed. In a few short hours, it was completely different. And every inch of it still sang with his touch. She was back where she started. Time had reversed itself, and she was living the past all over again.

Dylan lay for a moment with his eyes closed, letting the miracle sink into his bones. Lord, he felt good. Stretching, he turned his head toward her.

But she wasn't there. Something hard and painful gripped his chest, making each breath an effort. He stumbled to his feet and grabbed his jeans, pulling them on as he rushed out of the room.

It took five minutes for him to realize she wasn't in the house. Pulling the front door open, he walked out and stood on the porch, rapidly scanning the area. Perspiration beaded his upper lip when he saw nothing, no movement. He took all four steps at once, then stopped abruptly when he saw footprints in the dew. She had left a clear trail that led into the woods to the east of the house.

Back inside the house, he pulled on his shirt, not bothering to button it as he stepped into his shoes and again went outside.

Dylan had gone almost a quarter of a mile into the woods when he found her. She stood leaning against a tree as she stared at the sky through a break in the branches overhead. Although twigs crackled under his feet, she didn't look in his direction.

Dylan wanted to grab her by the shoulders and shake her for throwing him into a panic, but he didn't. He couldn't. Something had changed. She looked fragile this morning. She looked so damned fragile.

He moved slowly toward her. "Any trees slap you silly?" he asked when he was a foot away.

A smile twitched at her lips, then faded. "Not yet. I think I was wrong about them." She pushed away from the tree. "There are other houses around here . . . probably close. I smelled smoke a minute ago." She shook her head. "I don't know why we didn't think of it last night."

Dylan's fingers clenched into fists. She was running scared. She was going to pretend that nothing had happened between them. He wanted to tell her to stop it. He wanted to tell her not to try to cancel out something important, something beautiful, by pretending it hadn't happened. But he didn't say anything. He was too much of a coward.

"We could do that, couldn't we?" she asked, her voice still nervous. "We could walk to a neighbor's house and use the telephone."

"Yes, we could do that, but why don't we have breakfast first?" He reached out to touch her wildly curling hair but let his hand fall back to his side. "You haven't even combed your hair," he said gently.

"Haven't I?" She touched her hair and smiled. "It's a good thing I didn't run into anyone. I probably would have started a legend. The Wild Woman of upstate New York. I don't mind people thinking I'm wild, but I wouldn't want them to think I'm a Yankee."

"They wouldn't think that. They would look at you and fall in love," he whispered. "They would want to hold you, to protect you."

Keely heard the words and she heard the tone. The gentleness spread through her, making her weak.

"Do you—" She broke off and moistened her lips. "Do you want to protect me?"

He nodded.

"Then, please—" She blinked twice as helpless tears gathered in her eyes. "Please get me away from here. I want to go home. I want to go where it's—"

"Safe?"

She nodded frantically.

When he put his arm around her shoulders, she leaned against him, needing his strength. "I want to go home, Dylan," she said again.

"I'm sorry . . . I'm so damn sorry," he whispered. "If it would help, I would do anything in my power to make it go away, but don't you see, Keely, there's nothing either of us can do? We could ignore it for a thousand years, and it would still be there. Baby, look at me." He held her face between his hands and held her head still so that she had to look at him. "It happened, Keely. We made love. Last night, in front of the fireplace, we touched and we kissed and we made each other happy."

She moved her face out of his hands and pushed it into his shoulder. "It shouldn't have happened. It can't happen again. It can't."

With a sound of rough desperation, she pulled away from him and tried to walk away, but he wouldn't let her. He grasped her arm and held her there.

"We can't wipe out the past." His voice was no longer calm. He sounded as desperate as she felt. "I wish to God I could, but it doesn't work that way. I can't take back all the times I hurt you. I can't take back all the times I disappointed you. I can't."

"Not just you," she said, shaking her head. "I said things that . . . I did things—" She broke off and shook her head again.

"Yes, you said things and you did things and

you hurt me. We hurt each other. We can't change that now. It's over. We've got to let it go and get on with our lives."

"That's what I was trying to do," she whispered.

"Without me." His voice was shaking with intensity. "You've been trying to do it without me."

"And you haven't?"

"I tried. I tried real hard. But it didn't work. I can't see you without wanting you. Keely, we've been fooling ourselves. We've both been fighting what we feel because we don't want to get tangled up again. It was stupid and useless. I don't know about you, but I couldn't be more involved if we had made love four or five times a day for the last six months. I'm hooked. I'm hooked on the way you smell, the way you laugh. I'm hooked on the way I feel when you touch me."

She kept shaking her head. She didn't want to hear what he was saying. She didn't want to admit she felt the same way. She didn't want him to know that if she never saw him again, she would still carry the essence of him inside her forever.

"Why don't we give it another shot, Keely?"

She froze. "What? What did you say?" she asked in a hoarse whisper.

"I said why don't we take it from here and see what happens? We can't go on like this, sliding around in purgatory. Let's take charge again. And it will either be an end . . . or a new beginning. Either way, we're better off than we are now."

"Do you know what you're asking?" Her eyes were wide with fear. "Do you realize what kind of chance we would be taking?"

"Isn't taking chances what life's all about? Look . . . Come on, dammit, look at me."

She did, and the moment their eyes met, she was confused. Perspiration glistened on his face, and his eyes held a strange, hunted look.

"What we had last night, is that worth taking a chance on?" His throat muscles rippled as he swallowed. After a moment he whispered, "Am *I* worth taking a chance on?"

There was something there, she told herself. There was something in his face, something in his eyes, that she should pay attention to.

But she couldn't think. She had to concentrate. He was asking her a question. Was last night worth taking a chance on? The risks were incredibly high. If she had to go through it all again, would she survive?

Suddenly she realized she was asking herself the wrong question. What she should be asking herself was, could she let it end? If they left, if she ran back to Dallas, would that finish it? Would she be able to stay away from him, knowing that he still wanted her?

There was no decision to make. It had been made the night before, when he showed her how much he needed her. No matter what happened, no matter what the future held, she would never have the strength to walk away from him. Like the fool she was, she would wait until he, once again, decided he didn't want her anymore.

She raised her head to meet his eyes. White lines of tension bordered his mouth, and she reached up to touch them. "I guess you'd better deal me in," she whispered.

He threw his head back, his eyes closed as he drew in a deep, shaky breath; then, without opening his eyes, he pulled her into his arms, and for a long time he simply held her. When she felt his body tremble, she almost cried out, touched in a way she had never before been touched. She wanted desperately to make things right. She ached to pull him away from whatever terror had him in its grip. Acting instinctively, she framed his face with her hands, spreading eager kisses across his face.

It seemed to be the signal he was waiting for, because his hands began moving quickly, hungrily, over her back and hips, pulling her closer and even closer, so that her body fit tightly against his.

"I don't think I can wait until we get back to the house," he groaned, his touch becoming more urgent. "I need you now, Keely."

"I know . . . I know," she whispered.

He slid the zipper of her jumpsuit down to her waist and spread his warm fingers across her breast. "Did I tell you how much I missed your breasts? Did I tell you how much I missed the way you catch your breath when I touch you here?"

Sliding his arms under the open jumpsuit, he moved her body so that her aching nipples brushed against his chest. He shoved one leg between her thighs, pressing, rubbing, driving her crazy with the friction brought by his movements.

"Dylan . . . please," she gasped, digging her fingers into his back. "I can't take much more."

She slid one hand between them, trying to get at the snap of his jeans. When he felt the movement, he pulled off the flannel shirt and unfastened his jeans, watching her as she slid the zipper all the way down. Then, with a slight shrug of her shoulders, the jumpsuit fell to the ground around her feet.

He stared at her for a moment, then went down on his haunches to spread out the flannel shirt. Keely dropped to her knees behind him. She snaked her arms around his waist and pressed her throbbing breasts against his back.

"I don't need that," she murmured. "I don't need anything except you."

He reached behind him and lifted her, lowering her down on the shirt. "The ground is still partially frozen."

Grasping his neck, she drew him toward her, closer and closer. "I won't feel it. I won't feel anything but . . . this," she whispered just as their lips met.

The emotional intensity had built in her until she felt almost at the breaking point. She felt as though she had barely missed a disaster, and the adrenaline released heightened every sensation. His every touch went right to the heart of her, pulling her toward fulfillment. And when she reached it, it was rapture on a different scale. It was more brilliant, more poignant, than any climax that had come before.

And there was something else. Something that shook her loose from reality. Always before, when they made love, they had mentally separated at the last second, each reaching the final pleasure on his or her own, as individuals. But this time they went together, as one. It wasn't a matter of timing. It was an intimate affinity that shouldn't have been possible. But it happened. It happened, and it bound them.

"Dylan?" Keely murmured a long time later.

"Mmm?" His voice sounded lazy, contented.

"Would you do me a favor?"

"Anything. You want the moon? You want my checkbook? You want me to vote Republican?"

"Maybe later," she said. "Right now I want you to roll me over and see if frostbite has set in."

He chuckled. "Reality returns," he said as he moved off her. He rolled her over and began rubbing her back and buttocks briskly. "Better?"

"The feeling's coming back," she said, rising to her feet to step into the jumpsuit.

But he wouldn't let her zip it all the way up. He insisted that she leave it open to the waist so he could touch her. For some strange reason, Keely was in no mood to argue.

"What happens now?" she asked. Although she was reluctant to ask the question, she needed to know what she had got herself into. "Do we wait for Cody to come back? Do we go to a neighbor's house and call a mechanic? And what about when we get back to Dallas? I mean, are we going to start dating, or what?"

He smoothed a kiss up her throat and across her cheek. "I thought, if it's all right with you, that we would spend a few days together. Away somewhere, just the two of us."

"Like where?"

He glanced around. "What about here? You like the house, don't you?"

"I love it, but . . . you and Cody must be *real* good friends," she said slowly.

He laughed. "I found Cody's appointment book last night. He's in Europe at a new gallery. He'll be gone a couple of weeks."

"You found out last night?"

"I was going to tell you, but I got . . . distracted."

"I'll accept that," she said, snuggling against him. "But we can't be stuck out here. We'll have to get the car fixed. How far—"

She broke off and studied the look in his eyes. "What did you do? Dylan Tate, you answer me. What did you do? There's a telephone, isn't there? You hid the stupid telephone. You low-down—"

"No," he said, shaking his head and laughing. "There is no telephone."

"Then what?"

"Well, see, it was like this. Last night when I was getting the crackers and cheese, I saw it was getting late, and I figured Cody probably wouldn't be coming home, because he hates to drive in the dark. And that's when it occurred to me that we needed to spend some . . . I guess you could say, some quality time together, so I . . ."

"So you what?" she asked, exasperation growing. "Don't stop in the middle. You did what?"

"I pulled a little wire out of the distributor."

He studied her face for a while. "Keely? Honey, are you mad at me?"

She shot a glance at him. Just as she had suspected, his eyes were sparkling with amusement. "You don't give a damn if I'm mad or not."

"Of course I do. Are you?"

"You know how I feel about being manipulated."

He nodded slowly. "I know."

"And you know how I feel about being lied to."

"I didn't exactly lie. I just didn't mention that the car wouldn't start because I had pulled that little wire."

She snorted in contempt. "Lie or not, it was devious. You know how I feel about people being devious."

He rubbed his chin. "No," he said slowly. "No, I don't think you've ever told me how you feel about devious people."

"I think they're not to be trusted. I think they're lower than the stuff that grows between the tiles in the bathroom. I think—" Her lips twitched against her will. "I think they're kind of cute with moldy leaves in their hair."

He pulled her into his arms, laughing as they fell back on the semi-thawed ground.

Nine

The next two days were full ones for Keely and Dylan. Since they had brought nothing with them, they purchased clothes in the little town they had passed through on the first day. The clothes weren't fashionable, but fashion wasn't important.

Touching was. Touching, kissing, and simply being together were all right at the top of the list.

Most of their time was spent in a big feather bed, making love, trying to catch up. Sometimes their lovemaking was filled with laughter and teasing; sometimes desperate hunger and lonely memories moved them. But always, whatever the mood, their coming together was wonderful.

When they weren't making love, they were talking. They would sit in the feather bed and talk for hours. Dylan finally seemed to understand that it was important for her to know about him, about his past.

He told her about his troubled life with his father, an unfeeling sort of man who had thrown Dylan out of the house when the latter was in the throes of teenage rebellion.

"I don't blame him," Dylan had told her. "I had a smart mouth and a bad attitude. I would have kicked me out too."

Dylan had assured her that he held no grudges against his father. There were no bad feelings, he said. But what bothered Keely was that he seemed to have no feelings, good or bad, for his father. He could have been talking about a stranger.

It was more difficult for him to talk about his mother. Keely was careful to keep away from the subject of Mary Tate's death. She encouraged him to talk about the happy times. Keely got the impression that his mother had been a gentle woman, fragile physically and emotionally. She tried to pull up sympathy for the woman, and if it had been anyone else, Keely could have managed it. But it wasn't anyone else. It was a woman who had wounded the child Dylan had been and the man he had become. Keely wasn't sure she would ever be able to forgive Mary Tate.

Although Dylan shared his past, his memories, with Keely, she knew there were still things he was holding back. She could see in his face when it was time to stop talking. She didn't push him. She would take it one step at a time. Just the fact that he was finally talking gave her hope that this time would be different.

On the evening of their third day together, they had dinner in town. Like most small towns, this one shut down early. The little diner where they ate was the only place open. Over dinner, they watched customers come and go, speculating quietly on occupations and relationships, laughing softly as the speculations got out of hand.

When they had finished dessert, Keely stood up and walked to the jukebox to study the selection. If they were going to have a night on the town, they might as well do it right. She loved music and had missed having it around in the last few days.

Before she had made a choice, she felt movement beside her and glanced up. A pleasant-looking older man stood beside her. She and Dylan had watched him earlier. Dylan said the man was single, worked in the hardware store, and was in town because his mother nagged him when he was home.

"I hope you like country music," the man said, his voice casually friendly. "And your tastes have to be conservative. Around here we consider Willie Nelson an upstart."

Keely laughed. "I noticed."

"My name is Sam Adkins. I saw you and your friend in town a couple of days ago."

"It's nice to meet you, Sam." She held out her hand. "I'm Keely Durant, and my 'friend' is—" She broke off. They might be conservative, but even here people had probably heard of Dylan Tate. "My friend is Dylan," she said finally.

"I hope you both enjoyed your meal . . . my wife's the cook." He smiled. "If I want a decent meal, I have to come to town for it."

"You don't work in town?" she asked, storing the information so she could use it to humiliate Dylan.

He shook his head. "I have a small farm. I spend a lot of my time here, waiting." He grinned. "Sometimes I even think she's worth it."

"At least you have company while you wait. It's a chance for you to visit with your neighbors."

He shook his head slightly. "They're a little stand-offish with newcomers."

"You haven't lived here long?"

"Not long enough," he said ruefully. "My folks moved here when I was three, about forty-five years ago."

"You're exaggerating," she accused.

"Not much. Most of the families around here have been here for generations. When they talk about the war, you're never sure whether they mean World War One, World War Two, or the Revolutionary War."

She laughed when she saw the look on his face. "And I thought it was bad in Tomball. I don't think—"

"Find anything?"

Swinging around, she found Dylan standing directly behind her. She smiled, catching his hand in hers. "No, not yet. Dylan, this is—"

"Are you ready to leave?" He turned his hand

over, holding her fingers in a tight grasp. "We can find some music on the car radio."

Ten minutes later, Keely was still fuming. She sat beside him in the car, holding her body stiff as she stared straight ahead.

"Okay, Keely, spill your guts," he said. "Tell me what's eating you."

She answered immediately, her voice tight. "You were rude. Rude and boorish. You didn't even wait to let me introduce Sam. You acted like he wasn't even there."

"I felt no need to get to know *Sam*."

His contemptuous tone had her clenching her fists in her lap. "I had forgotten. I forgot how sometimes you can act like an ill-mannered, ill-tempered clod."

"And I forgot that sometimes you get overly friendly," he ground out.

"It was always my fault, wasn't it? When I'm with you, the rest of the world is not supposed to exist. There but for the grace of God goes God, Dylan Lord and Master Tate. You didn't even want me talking to Sally and Little Nikita when you weren't right beside me."

"Why is it such a big deal? Have you ever heard of constancy? Have you ever heard of dancing with the one that brung you?"

Frustrated, she hit the padded door with her fist. "That's crazy! You make it sound like I deserted you. I was simply being polite."

"You—" He broke off and drew in a long breath. "I'm sorry," he said, his voice stiff. "I'm sorry I acted like a clod. I'm sorry I have no manners. I'm sorry I opened my damn mouth."

"You don't sound sorry. You sound mad."

He shook his head. "If I'm mad, it's only at myself. I really am sorry, Keely. I won't do it again." He paused. After a moment he put a hand on her knee. "Okay?"

She bit her lip, still feeling hangover tension. Shaking her head, she raised her hand and covered his where it still rested on her knee. "Okay," she agreed.

Always before, she had thought the way he acted was because he was too critical of her and insensitive to the feelings of others. But tonight she was rethinking the problem. She wondered if there wasn't more to it. Why hadn't she realized before how possessive he was? She had always taken his criticism at face value. She had become angry and defensive instead of trying to see what was behind it.

For just a moment she allowed herself to feel pleasure in the knowledge that he cared enough to be possessive, but she very quickly squelched the pleasure. Jealousy didn't mean love. A man could want to possess something without loving it. Maybe he was on an ego trip and simply believed he deserved every second of her attention.

Somehow, she thought that wasn't the answer. In fact, it seemed to be the opposite. As ridiculous as it sounded, she realized Dylan was insecure. She didn't know why. She didn't know whether it was the relationship or something in him alone.

But the more she thought, the more she believed she had found the answer.

"Don't think so much," he said suddenly. "It makes me nervous."

His voice was light, but there was an underlying inflection that eluded her. She wanted to talk to him about the evening, her conclusions. She wanted to ask him what motivated him, but she didn't. Being together again was too new. She didn't want to dive into deep water until she was sure they wouldn't sink.

"Okay," she said. "Let's talk. Name a subject, any subject, and I'll dazzle you with my knowledge."

"You don't have to talk to dazzle me. I'm easy. Just cut your eyes at me like you did over dessert, and I'll be as dazzled as they come."

She laughed huskily. "If I cut my eyes at you all the way home, I'll end up cross-eyed."

"I'll accept a compromise. Let's talk about what we're going to do tonight with no television and no radio for entertainment."

"I guess we'll have to find some other way of amusing ourselves," she said.

"Such as?"

She put her hand on his thigh, moving it lightly across the denim-covered muscle. "We could always make shadow pictures on the wall. Have I ever shown you my bald eagle?"

He cleared his throat. "You show me yours and I'll show you mine."

She leaned against him, laughing softly. It was

going to be all right, she told herself. They would work out all the problems. They had to.

Dylan lay in the big feather bed in Cody's blue guest room. Keely was asleep beside him. He almost envied her. He hadn't had much sleep in the last three days. He was afraid to sleep, afraid he would wake up again and find her gone.

When he thought of the argument they had had on the way home, he winced and cursed himself for being such a fool. He knew he couldn't hold on to her like that. She didn't like it. He should have remembered.

In the future, he would have to keep a tight rein on himself. He didn't want her to feel he was watching her every move, gauging her every mood. Even if he was.

It was going to work this time, he told himself as he lay in the darkness. He wouldn't let either of them go through that hell again. From now on, he would be Mr. Sweetness and Light. He would be any damn thing Keely wanted him to be. And he would keep up the act for the rest of his life, if it would keep her with him.

Keely and Dylan spent the next day wandering in and out of antique shops. Keely couldn't believe the things she found, beautiful pieces that would have cost a fortune in Texas, if they had been available at all.

After a lot of good-natured dickering, Dylan bought her a beautiful silver bowl and a blue porcelain pitcher. She let him buy them because both items were bargains, and because he wanted so badly to give them to her.

Early in the afternoon they drove to the river. Keely hadn't known it was nearby, but she learned very soon that in this part of the country most of the farmland was in river valleys for the simple reason that it was the only space flat enough to farm.

They ate their picnic lunch on the bank of the beautiful, slow-moving waterway. They lay on a blanket in the sun, talking and eating and talking some more. There on that blanket, it felt like spring. It wasn't a Texas spring. It was more tentative, more cautious, than what Keely was used to. But it brought all the nostalgia, all the keenly felt emotions, of spring everywhere on earth.

"Or maybe it's just indigestion," Dylan said when she told him how the day made her feel.

"It's not indigestion. I never have indigestion, and I never have gas."

"Is that right? Why?"

She rolled over, resting the upper part of her body against his chest. "Because when He made me, God decided He would make the perfect human. A lean, mean loving machine."

He smothered his laughter against her neck. "I can vouch for the mean part." He grasped her hips with both his hands. "Lean? I would have said skinny, but I guess God knows best."

She grabbed a plastic fork and held it against his throat. "Skinny? Do you still say skinny, Mr. Superstar?"

"I meant smooth and curvy," he said, shaking with laughter. "I might even have meant voluptuous."

She threw down the fork and kissed him on the cheek. "Count yourself lucky. By this much"—with her forefinger and thumb she measured half an inch of air—"you missed being a victim of the Texas Plastic Fork Massacre."

"We're in New York."

"That's another reason you missed it."

When they finally returned to the house, it was dark. The day had been long, filled with secret, necessary caresses. Keely was hungry for him. And he knew. Dylan didn't miss much.

When they walked into the house, he didn't pause in the entryway. He grabbed her hand and made straight for the stairs.

An hour later, she held his head against her breast as she slowly stroked his hair. Then, slowly, inexorably, he began to move away. When he was several inches from her, he moved through a streak of moonlight, and Keely saw his features clearly.

She stared, her eyes wide open, as pain clutched at her, choking her. It was there again. The withdrawal was there in his face, damnable, unmistakable. She felt icy fingers of fear clutch her heart, and the coldness spread outward from there, until not an inch of her was left untouched.

In a frantic, mindless panic, she scrambled from the bed. She wouldn't scream, she told herself. She wouldn't cry. Her chest hurt with the effort, but she didn't make a sound.

She hated him. At that moment, she hated Dylan more than she had ever hated anything or anyone in her life. He had made promises. He had pulled her in, giving her hope, only to do it to her again.

My God, why wasn't he laughing? she wondered fiercely. A bigger fool than she was didn't exist. Someone should be there to enjoy it.

Moving awkwardly toward the door, she said stiffly, "I'm going to take a bath."

She had her hand on the doorknob when a hand grasped her forearm and she was spun around to face him. Violent anger twisted the features she had seen so clearly in the moonlight. She closed her eyes, knowing she wasn't going to be spared any of it. It was all going to happen again.

"What is it?" His voice was tense and hoarse. "What in hell is it? Why do you look at me like that? Son of a bitch, Keely, how much do you think I can take? I tried . . . You owe me, dammit. At the very least, you owe me an explanation. You stay right where you are and you tell me what you see in me that makes you look like that."

She jerked her arm away and backed against the door. "Let it go, Dylan. Just . . . just let it go."

"No! Not again. You're not going to slink off and

build that stupid, impenetrable shell around you. Not this time. This time you're going to explain. This time you're going to tell me the truth."

She dragged in a shaky breath. "You want war? Fine, you'll get it. Let me tell you what I see in your face. I see nothing. Do you hear me . . . *nothing!* At least, nothing for me." She pushed a frantic hand through her hair. "Give it another shot, you said. Well, we gave it the old college try, Dylan. And nothing has changed. It's just like the last time." She shook her head and whispered, "Just like the last time."

Clenching his fists, he swung away from her. "Just like the last time," he repeated. "I should have known. I was crazy to think it would be any different."

"We were both crazy."

Keely silently blessed the anger that gripped her. Anger shoved the pain deep inside her. Anger held her upright. Anger took over her brain and her tongue.

"I thought that if I could find out what your childhood was like, I would understand," she said. "I thought I would be able to get under your skin and find out what makes you act the way you do. But it's not about the past, is it? With you, it's the past, present, and the future. I can see why your father kicked you out. Like you said, Dylan, there are certain things you can't blame on other people. You have to take responsibility for them yourself."

"So what are you saying?" he asked.

"I'm saying that what's wrong with us can't be fixed by digging into the past. Because it's the 'us' part that's wrong. We don't work. It's a fact, and there's nothing we can do to change it. We're bad for each other."

As she talked, Keely had been silently begging him to deny it. She had been pleading with him to tell her she was wrong. That it wasn't happening again. That he wasn't turning away from her . . . again.

But he didn't. He didn't say anything for a long time. Finally his shoulders moved stiffly. "You're not being honest, Keely. I'm sick of tiptoeing around the real issue. Let's get it out in the open. It isn't us. It's me. Isn't that what you wanted to say? We're not bad for each other. *I'm* bad for *you*. I don't work for you. Little Miss Muffet is too sweet and pure for the dirty old Street Rat."

His sarcastic, mocking voice reached her, and something exploded in her mind. She rushed toward him and slammed her fist into his shoulder. "Shut up," she spat at him when he turned around. "Just shut the hell up! You always make fun of me. You mock how I was raised and where I was born. You've accused me of being smug and stuck-up and backward. Well, who the hell gave you the right to judge? You practically grew up on the street, but I've never called you trash."

She raised her fist to hit him again, but he grasped her wrist and held it tightly. "Haven't you?" he whispered, his voice harsh. "Haven't you, Keely?"

Her head jerked back as though he had slapped her. She moistened her lips and shook her head in violent denial. "No," she rasped out. "No, you're wrong. I never. Never."

When he released her wrist, she fell against the wall. She couldn't stop shaking. "Why do we do this?" she whispered. "My God, Dylan, why do we always do this? I can't take any more. I just can't take any more."

"No." His voice was weak, as though he had been sapped of strength. "Neither can I. Come on, let's get our things together and get the hell out of here."

Ten

Two weeks after flying back from New York, Keely sat at the small desk in her apartment as she worked on the article about Dylan. She picked up her coffee cup but had to put it back down when her hand began to tremble. She needed to eat something, but the thought of food made her sick.

When the doorbell rang, her heart lurched. It wasn't Dylan, she told herself sternly. He wouldn't ever come near her again.

It was Celeste. She took one look at Keely and started swearing. She grabbed Keely's hand and pulled her into the kitchen.

"Sit," Celeste ordered. She reached into the refrigerator and pulled out a carton of milk, smelled it, then poured a glass full. "Drink this while I fix you a sandwich."

Keely stared at the milk.

"It's not going to do anything, Keely. It's milk. It's good for you. Drink it."

Keely glanced up. "I think I might throw up if I drink it."

Celeste stopped spreading peanut butter on a slice of bread. "Are you pregnant?"

Keely laughed, then pressed a hand against her mouth to stop the hysterical sound. "No."

"Good. That complication you don't need." She slammed the sandwich down in front of Keely. "Eat."

Celeste waited, drumming her fingers against the table, while Keely ate. When the last piece of bread and the last sip of milk were gone, she put the saucer and the glass in the sink, then turned around and leaned against the cabinet. "Now tell me what it's going to take to snap you out of this."

"Dylan," Keely said automatically.

"You had him."

Keely shook her head. "He . . . He—"

"So what you're saying is you want Dylan, but only the way *you* want him to be, not the way he is."

"You make me sound like a selfish pig." Keely leaned her head on her folded arms. "Maybe it is selfish. Maybe I should have been willing to take what I could get. I don't know. I just know I can't sleep at night thinking of the way he looked at me. I swear he hated me. I couldn't live with that.

It would kill me, Celeste. Sooner or later, it would kill me."

"And just what do you think you're doing to yourself?" her friend asked in disgust. "There are easier ways to commit suicide. Either have the guts to jump off a bridge, or get on with your life."

Celeste was trying to make her mad, but it didn't work. Keely knew her friend too well. She wasn't angry or disgusted with Keely. She was worried.

Keely smiled. "I'll be all right. It's bad right now, but—" She broke off, then continued in a whisper, "Sometimes I feel myself falling asleep, and I think, Thank God, now I can get some rest. I'll start drifting off, then suddenly I see his face. I see the way he looked when he pulled away from me. My heart starts pounding, and I can't catch my breath. The pain here"—she touched her chest—"is so bad." She pressed her lips together in an effort to make them stop trembling. "I wish it would stop hurting."

Keely pulled herself upright and wiped her eyes. "I'm sorry. I really am going to be all right." She laughed softly. "I should be an old pro by now. I've been through it before. Practice is supposed to make perfect."

"The bastard," Celeste ground out. "The dirty bastard."

Keely shook her head with quick, jerky movements. "I told you. It's just chemistry. Put us together and we explode. And I wasn't the only one in trouble. He was hurting too. I could see it in his face, right there at the end. I didn't know what to do. I didn't know how to make it go away." She tightened her fingers into fists. "There's something in me that torments him. I knew it, and I hated it, so I hit him. I hit him and I screamed at him. I'm a real prize."

She looked away from the tears in Celeste's eyes and rose to her feet. "I've got to get back to work. Thanks for the sandwich . . . and the shoulder."

"Keely, why don't I stay with you for a while? I'll grab my sleeping bag and camp out in your living room. We can have slumber parties every night."

Keely shook her head. "You're a good friend—I don't think I've ever had a better one—but it's not necessary. I told you, I've been through it before. This doesn't last forever." She smiled. "It only seems like forever."

Henry glanced up from the page and looked her squarely in the eyes. "Garbage," he said succinctly.

"Come on, Henry, don't beat around the bush," Keely said, her voice dry. "Tell me what you really think of it."

"What in hell's wrong with you?" he asked, leaning toward her. "You've never in your life turned in anything like this. This is the most important assignment you've ever had, and you hand me this piece of trash. It's nothing more than a list of facts. There's no emotion, no insight, no guts. Nothing that gives you a real feel for what the man's like. You're not writing for *The World Book*.

This is supposed to hold the reader's attention, not put him to sleep."

Keely bit her lip. Thank goodness she had got past the weepy stage. Henry didn't allow tears in his office.

She reached across the desk and took the pages from him. "I'll have something else for you in three days."

"You'll have something for me tomorrow. And it better be damn good."

She nodded and stood up.

"Keely?"

He spoke just as she was pulling open the door. She glanced over her shoulder to find him staring at her, a frown pulling his brows together.

"I'm counting on you. The magazine needs this article. It needs you."

Now he was gentle with her, she thought in exasperation, feeling unwelcome tears burn her eyes. Without looking at him, she nodded and left his office.

Keely didn't stop at her desk. She walked out of the building and headed for her car. In her apartment she dropped her purse without pausing and sat down at the little desk in her living room. She fed a sheet of paper into the typewriter and began to type.

Keely lay back in a padded recliner beside the pool at her apartment complex. The flesh left bare by her bikini was sticking to the plastic pad, but she didn't care. It was her vacation, and she didn't have to care about anything if she didn't want to.

It wasn't the vacation she had scheduled earlier in the year, but Henry had insisted she take two weeks off. He said she was beginning to look like something his dog would try to bury in the backyard.

The magazine featuring her article had hit the stands two days earlier. Celeste and Wayne both said it was the best thing Keely had ever done. Neither of them met her eyes when they said it. Henry also said it was the best thing she had ever done. He wouldn't look her in the eye either.

She let her eyelids drift down. In the three days she had been off, she had managed to turn everything off. No thinking. No feeling. No hurting. Why did peace suddenly seem so empty?

When she felt something blocking the sun, she opened her eyes. Dylan stood beside the recliner, staring down at her. Without speaking, she closed her eyes again, her features never changing.

"I read the article."

"Are you going to sue?" she asked, her voice calm.

He laughed. "No. You didn't say a single nasty thing about me. Not even some that deserved to be said."

She swung her legs around and sat up. "What do you want, Dylan? You didn't come here to talk about the article."

"No," he agreed. "I was coming anyway, but the article gave me the courage to come sooner."

She shot a glance at him. "Why did you need courage? Were you afraid I would throw something at you?"

He shook his head, smiling. A moment later, he sat beside her on the recliner. "You made me sound like a decent guy in this." He nodded toward the magazine in his hand.

"I didn't want to disillusion your fans."

"Is that why you wrote it?"

She sighed. "No, I only told the truth. There's no hidden reason. It's my job."

He was silent for a moment. "The way this reads—" He broke off and cleared his throat. "The words you wrote, the way you talked about me . . . it almost sounds as if you care."

You thick-headed idiot, she fumed silently. If he had read the article, then he should have known it didn't read as if she cared. It read as if she loved him more than life. That was why Celeste and Wayne and Henry couldn't look at her. She hadn't exposed Dylan's vulnerabilities. She had exposed her own. Her heart was spread all over the pages of a magazine.

"So what's your point?"

"Do you?"

She closed her eyes, then opened them again. "That's an asinine question. I lived with you for two years. I got stomped on and came back for more. What do you think?"

"Would you look at me, Keely?"

She shook her head. "No."

He put his hand on her chin and turned her

head toward him with gentle pressure. "We need to talk."

"We talked in New York," she said stiffly.

"No . . . no, we didn't really. Don't you get the feeling that something is going on here, something we can't see because we're caught in the middle of it? In New York we yelled at each other, and we waltzed around a lot of things, but we didn't really talk." He paused and rubbed a rough hand across his jaw. "This is important to me, Keely. No matter what happens, even if you never let me near you again, I need to know. So now, while we're calm, would you tell me why you looked at me the way you did that last night? Would you tell me what I did to . . . to disgust you?"

She felt a wave of dizziness sweep over her. "Disgust?" She shook her head. "I don't know what you saw in my face, but it wasn't that. It couldn't have been that. Not in a million years."

He inhaled slowly. "Maybe that was too strong. Disappointment? Disillusionment?"

"I don't know . . . maybe." She moistened her lips in a nervous gesture. "I wanted so badly for—"

He picked up her hand. "I won't let it hurt you again. I promise. Just . . . please tell me. Tell me what I did, what I keep doing, to make you turn away from me. It's driving me crazy, wondering. I thought this time I could be what you wanted. I thought if I watched every move I made and every word I said, if I made sure the . . . the bad part of me, the part you hate . . . I thought if that part stayed buried, maybe I could keep you this time."

It was there again, she thought, frowning. That thing in his voice she had heard before, that deep, desperate insecurity.

"Did you think you had to be someone different to make me stay?" she asked, her voice incredulous.

"Didn't I?" He smiled wryly. "Every time the real Dylan popped up, you started pulling away from me."

She shook her head. "Celeste said the same thing. That I only wanted you if you would be what I wanted you to be. But it's not true. If you're talking about the arguments—Dylan, I wasn't pulling away from you. Everyone argues, even people in love."

He stood up abruptly, shoving his hands in his pockets. "I thought we were going to be honest. Or can't you admit it even to yourself?" He gave a harsh laugh. "I know what I am, Keely. I know someone like you couldn't love someone like me. I've always known. But we had something good together. I just want to know what I did to screw it up."

She stood up too. "This is it," she whispered tightly. "This is what I kept hearing in your voice in New York. This is what I couldn't quite get a grasp on. You don't think anyone can love you. You don't think you're worthy of love."

"Oh, please," he said, his voice sarcastic. "Don't you think I read? I know all about that psychological trash. Because my father was a cold bastard, because my mother committed suicide, I'm supposed to be blaming myself. I'm supposed to think it all happened because I wasn't good enough. Don't you think I went over all that stuff after we split, when I was looking for anything to give me a clue? Dammit, this is not in my mind! There is something in me that makes you turn away, and I want to know what the hell it is!" He swung around so that she only saw his stiff back. "God in heaven, I'd burn it out of my brain if I thought it would make you love me."

She raised her hand to touch him, but he must have sensed the movement, because he stepped just out of reach.

"I didn't come here to beg," he said. "I just came to get some answers."

She stepped forward and grasped his shoulder, giving it a violent jerk to turn him around. "But not give any? Why in hell didn't you ever tell me you love me?" she ground out. "Was this another of those little secrets you were keeping? When were you going to tell me? Were you ever going to tell me? Answer me, damn you!"

He stared at the tears on her face. He frowned, his eyes confused. "I—" He shook his head. "You had to know."

"How in hell would I know? Should I have known by the way you walked out on me five years ago? Was I supposed to figure it out when you stayed out all night then came home in those hideous black moods? Should I—"

She broke off abruptly, backing away from him. "Oh, no," she whispered, her eyes narrowing. "What are you trying to do to me, Dylan? You come here pretending you care, pretending you *love me*, pretending you want my love." She laughed, covering her mouth with her fingers. "My Lord, you almost had me again."

She drew in a deep breath. "You say you want answers, well, listen up. What you saw in my face in New York was pain. Pure and simple. Pain all the way down to my toes, Dylan. Because I took a chance again and I lost again. Because you were pulling away from me again. It was as if you were saying, 'Don't ask for more than sex, Keely.' I was good enough to sleep with, but heaven help me if I asked for more." She shook her head vehemently. "You're not going to sucker me in again, Dylan. That was the last time. I'm through playing your games."

She picked up her wrap and walked away.

She had taken only two steps when he caught up with her. "Keely, wait. Please, just give me another minute . . . please."

She stopped, but she held herself stiff and stared straight ahead. When the silence drew out, she glanced at him.

He looked up and met her gaze. "Keely, for a minute . . . a little while ago we were almost talking. We were almost making progress. When you looked at me—" He broke off and swallowed with difficulty. "There was something there. But then you got mad. What happened?"

She didn't want to talk anymore. She wanted to get into her apartment so she could fall apart in privacy.

"I remembered the black moods," she said quietly. "Sally said you didn't have them before we met, and you didn't have them after we broke up." She tried to smile, but she couldn't make her lips work. "That's not a good sign, Dylan. It's no good talking about love. I loved you back then, and look where it got us. Look what it did to both of us."

"Back then?" he whispered hoarsely.

She raised her gaze to the sky, then straightened her back. "Okay, why not? I loved you then. I loved you for the five years we were apart. I loved you in New York, and I love you now. I love you in spite of everything—the black moods, the bad temper, the smart mouth. I would have taken anything you cared to dish out. But you stopped dishing," she finished quietly.

He didn't say anything. After a moment he turned around and walked away. The muscles in his back were visible through the knit shirt. His head was slightly bent.

She watched him for a moment, feeling a hot constriction in her chest and throat. Suddenly, without thinking, she ran after him.

"Dylan?" she said when she was two steps behind him.

He stopped walking, but he didn't respond. He didn't move. He merely held himself stiff and straight.

She moved until she stood in front of him. "Dylan?" she said again.

When he raised his head to look at her, she

caught her breath sharply. His face looked ravaged, and his gray eyes were swimming with tears.

"I—" The word was a hoarse croak. He shook
his head, tightening his lips until they were white.

She couldn't stand it. She wrapped her arms
around him, swaying back and forth as she
crooned, "Baby . . . please don't."

He pressed his face into her neck, holding her
tightly. "I didn't know," he whispered. "I swear I
didn't know. I had to leave you . . . don't you see?
I had to. I could please you in bed, but that was
all. I couldn't make you happy. God, Keely, you
were so unhappy . . . *so damned unhappy.*"

She felt all her muscles clench inward. "Like
your mother," she whispered in sudden, over-
whelming understanding. "And you couldn't do
anything to help."

He shuddered. "It was driving me crazy. That
was what the black moods were, Keely. You were
so good. So damned sweet. I couldn't match that.
I didn't know how to match that. The black moods
were frustration. Self-contempt. Then after I left—"

"Shh," she said. "You had it all wrong . . . Don't
talk about it if it hurts you."

"I want to tell you. I need to tell you."

She nodded, holding him closer. "Then tell me."

"After I made *Sligh,* it all got worse. Being without you was eating me alive. One night I was
sitting on a hill looking down on the city, and
something hit me. A genuine revelation. I saw, as
clear as day, what the rest of my life was going to
be like without you. It scared the hell out of me,

Keely. That's why I came back to Dallas." He shook his head. "I don't know, maybe I thought you would like Dylan the superstar better. Maybe I thought you would love him."

She leaned against him, and he leaned against her. They held each other. When the shaking stopped, when the emotional tide began to ease, Keely drew back her head to look up at him.

"Let me see if I've got this straight. What we're saying here is, you walked out five years ago because you didn't think I loved you, and I walked out in New York because I didn't think you loved me. Is that about it?"

He laughed, hugging her tighter. "I don't think I've ever met two stupider people."

She reached up to touch his face. "See how well we match?"

After a while, after they had kissed a while, she remembered and she shivered.

"What is it?" he asked.

"I thought no one could have had a worse time than I did after we split, but I was wrong. It can't happen again, Dylan. I can't stand the thought of your being hurt like that again. We've got to find a way to keep it from happening again."

"Just don't ever stop loving me," he said. "Don't ever stop, Keely."

"I couldn't. I tried and I couldn't. This time it has to be different. We'll do all the things we should have done the first time. We'll talk," she said firmly.

"We'll make commitments," he said. "We'll get married. We'll have kids and buy a condo."

"And we won't fight . . . ever," she said, moving into the kiss she saw coming her way.

Later, she sighed and opened her eyes, then she frowned. "A condo? How can you raise kids in a condo? Kids need a yard. Trees and grass and sand piles. I should have expected something like this from you. It's just like you to—"

Dylan laughed, his eyes sparkling as he scooped her up in his arms and carried her toward the apartment building.

THE EDITOR'S CORNER

1990. A new decade. I suspect that most of us who are involved in romance publishing will remember the 1980s as "the romance decade." During the past ten years we have seen a momentous change as Americans jumped into the romance business and developed the talent and expertise to publish short, contemporary American love stories. Previously the only romances of this type had come from British and Australian authors through the Canadian company, Harlequin Enterprises. That lonely giant, or monopoly, was first challenged in the early 1980s when Dell published Ecstasy romances under Vivien Stephens's direction; by Simon and Schuster, which established Silhouette romances (now owned by Harlequin); and by Berkley/Jove, which supported my brainchild, Second Chance at Love. After getting that line off to a fine start, I came to Bantam.

The times had grown turbulent by the middle of the decade. But an industry had been born. Editors who liked and understood romance had been found and trained. Enormous numbers of writers had been discovered and were flocking to workshops and seminars sponsored by the brand-new Romance Writers of America to acquire or polish their skills.

LOVESWEPT was launched with six romances in May 1983. And I am extremely proud of all the wonderful authors who've been with us through these seven years and who have never left the fold, no matter the inducements to do so. I'm just as proud of the LOVESWEPT staff. There's been very little turnover—Susann Brailey, Nita Taublib, and Elizabeth Barrett have been on board all along; Carrie Feron and Tom Kleh have been here a year and two years, respectively. I'm also delighted by you, our readers, who have so wholeheartedly endorsed every innovation we've dared to make—our authors publishing under their real names and including pictures and autobiographies in their books, and the Fan of the Month feature, which puts the spotlight on a person who represents many of our readers. And of course I thank you for all your kind words about the Editor's Corner.

Now, starting this new decade, we find there wasn't enough growth in the audience for romances and/or there was too much being published, so that most American publishers have left the arena. It is only big Harlequin and little LOVESWEPT. Despite our small size, we are as vigorous and hearty, excited and exuberant now as we were in the beginning. I can't wait to see what the next ten years bring. What LOVESWEPT innova-

(continued)

tions do you imagine I might be summarizing in the Editor's Corner as we head into the new *century*?

But now to turn from musings about the year 2000 to the very real pleasures of next month!

Let Iris Johansen take you on one of her most thrilling, exciting journeys to Sedikhan, read **NOTORIOUS,** LOVESWEPT #378. It didn't matter to Sabin Wyatt that the jury had acquitted gorgeous actress Mallory Thane of his stepbrother's murder. She had become his obsession. He cleverly gets her to Sedikhan and confronts her with a demand that she tell him the truth about her marriage. When she does, he refuses to believe her story. He will believe only what he can feel: primitive, consuming desire for Mallory. . . . Convinced that Mallory returns his passion, Sabin takes her in fiery and unforgettable moments. That's only the beginning of **NOTORIOUS,** which undoubtedly is going onto my list of all-time favorites from Iris. I bet you, too, will label this romance a keeper.

Here comes another of Gail Douglas's fabulous romances about the sisters, *The Dreamweavers,* whose stories never fail to enmesh me and hold me spellbound. In LOVESWEPT #379, **SOPHISTICATED LADY,** we meet the incredible jazz pianist Pete Cochrane. When he looks up from the keyboard into Lisa Sinclair's eyes, he is captivated by the exquisite honey-blonde. He begins to play Ellington's "Sophisticated Lady," and Ann is stunned by the potent appeal of this musical James Bond. These two vagabonds have a rocky road to love that we think you'll relish every step of the way.

What a delight to welcome back Jan Hudson with her LOVESWEPT #380, **ALWAYS FRIDAY.** Full of fun and laced with fire, **ALWAYS FRIDAY** introduces us to handsome executive Daniel Friday and darling Tess Cameron. From the very first, Tess knows that there's no one better to unstarch Dan's collars and teach him to cut loose from his workaholism. Dan fears he can't protect his free-spirited and sexy Tess from disappointment. It's a glorious set of problems these two confront and solve.

Next, in Peggy Webb's **VALLEY OF FIRE,** LOVESWEPT #381, you are going to meet a dangerous man. A very dangerous and exciting man. I'd be surprised if you didn't find Rick McGill, the best private investigator in Tupelo, Mississippi, the stuff that the larger-than-life Sam Spades are made of with a little Valentino thrown in. Martha Ann Riley summons all her courage to dare to play Bacall to Rick's Bogart. She wants to find her sister's gambler husband . . . and turns out to be Rick's

(continued)

perfect companion for a sizzling night in a cave, a wicked romp through Las Vegas. Wildly attracted, Martha Ann thinks Rick is the most irresistible scoundrel she's ever met . . . and the most untrustworthy! Don't miss **VALLEY OF FIRE!** It's fantastic.

Glenna McReynolds gives us her most ambitious and thrilling romance to date in LOVESWEPT #382, **DATELINE: KYDD AND RIOS.** Nobody knew more about getting into trouble than Nikki Kydd, but that talent had made her perfect at finding stories for Josh Rios, the daring photojournalist who'd built his career reporting the battles and betrayals of San Simeon's dictatorship. After three years as partners, when he could resist her no longer, he ordered Nikki back to the States—but in the warm, dark tropical night he couldn't let her go . . . without teaching the green-eyed witch her power as a woman. She'd vanished with the dawn rather than obey Josh's command to leave, but now, a year later, Nikki needs him back . . . to fulfill a desperate bargain.

What a treat you can expect from Fayrene Preston next month—the launch book of her marvelous quartet about the people who live and work in a fabulous house, SwanSea Place. Here in LOVESWEPT #383, *SwanSea Place:* **THE LEGACY,** Caitlin Deverell had been born in SwanSea, the magnificent family home on the wild, windswept coast of Maine, and now she was restoring its splendor to open it as a luxury resort. When Nico DiFrenza asked her to let him stay for a few days, caution demanded she refuse the mysterious visitor's request— but his spellbinding charm made that impossible! So begins a riveting tale full of the unique charm Fayrene can so wonderfully invent for us.

Altogether a spectacular start to the new decade with great LOVESWEPT reading.

Warm good wishes,

Carolyn Nichols

Carolyn Nichols
Editor
LOVESWEPT
Bantam Books
666 Fifth Avenue
New York, NY 10103

FAN OF THE MONTH

Hazel Parker

Twelve years ago my husband Hoke insisted that I quit my job as a data processor to open a paperback bookstore. The reason was that our book bill had become as large as our grocery bill. Today I am still in the book business, in a much larger store, still reading and selling my favorite romance novels.

My most popular authors are of course writing for what I consider to be the number one romance series—LOVESWEPT. One of the all-time favorites is Kay Hooper. Her books appeal to readers because of her sense of humor and unique characters (for instance, Pepper in **PEPPER'S WAY**). And few authors can write better books than Iris Johansen's **THE TRUST-WORTHY REDHEAD** or Fayrene Preston's **FOR THE LOVE OF SAMI.** When the three authors get together (as they did for the Delaney series), you have *dynamite.* Keep up the good work, LOVESWEPT.

THE DELANEY DYNASTY

Men and women whose loves an passions are so glorious it takes many great romance novels by three bestselling authors to tell their tempestuous stories.

THE SHAMROCK TRINITY

☐	21975	RAFE, THE MAVERICK *by Kay Hooper*	$2.95
☐	21976	YORK, THE RENEGADE *by Iris Johansen*	$2.95
☐	21977	BURKE, THE KINGPIN *by Fayrene Preston*	$2.95

THE DELANEYS OF KILLAROO

☐	21872	ADELAIDE, THE ENCHANTRESS *by Kay Hooper*	$2.75
☐	21873	MATILDA, THE ADVENTURESS *by Iris Johansen*	$2.75
☐	21874	SYDNEY, THE TEMPTRESS *by Fayrene Preston*	$2.75

THE DELANEYS: *The Untamed Years*

☐	21899	GOLDEN FLAMES *by Kay Hooper*	$3.50
☐	21898	WILD SILVER *by Iris Johansen*	$3.50
☐	21897	COPPER FIRE *by Fayrene Preston*	$3.50

Buy them at your local bookstore or use this page to order.

Bantam Books, Dept. SW7, 414 East Golf Road, Des Plaines, IL 60016

Please send me the items I have checked above. I am enclosing $_____
(please add $2.00 to cover postage and handling). Send check or money order, no cash or C.O.D.s please.

Mr/Ms _____

Address _____

City/State _____ Zip _____

SW7–11/89

Please allow four to six weeks for delivery.
Prices and availability subject to change without notice.

NEW!

Handsome Book Covers Specially Designed To Fit Loveswept Books

Our new French Calf Vinyl book covers come in a set of three great colors—royal blue, scarlet red and kachina green.

Each 7" × 9½" book cover has two deep vertical pockets, a handy sewn-in bookmark, and is soil and scratch resistant.

To order your set, use the form below.

THE LATEST IN BOOKS
AND AUDIO CASSETTES